ZAK

A Novel

True Blue SEALs Series

SHARON HAMILTON

BOOKS BY SHARON HAMILTON

SEAL BROTHERHOOD
SEAL Encounter (Book .5)

Accidental SEAL (Book 1)

SEAL Endeavor (Book 1.5)

Fallen SEAL Legacy (Book 2)

SEAL Under Covers (Book 3)

SEAL The Deal (Book 4)

Cruisin' For A SEAL (Book 5)

SEAL My Destiny (Book 6)

SEAL Of My Heart (Book 7)

BAD BOYS OF SEAL TEAM 3
SEAL's Promise (Book 1)

SEAL My Home (Book 2)

SEAL's Code (Book 3)

BAND OF BACHELORS
Lucas (Book 1)

Alex (Book 2)

TRUE BLUE SEALS
True Navy Blue (prequel to Zak)

Zak

AUTHOR'S NOTE

This is dedicated to all those who have loved once, twice, perhaps three times or more, and thought they should give up. I believe in Happily Ever Afters. I believe in long slow kisses and moonlit strolls on the beach. I believe in walks in the woods on sunny days. I believe in forgiveness and the healing power of true love.

Love hurts and makes us strong. I believe it brings us to the truest expression of ourselves, and when we strive for true love, we are striving for the very best within our souls.

Yes, even for Navy SEALs, *True Love Heals In The Gardens Of The Heart.*

Live well and love often. And let's explore the depths our hearts can take us, even in this very short ride of life.

authorsharonhamilton.com
sharonhamilton2001@gmail.com

I support two main charities: Navy SEAL/UDT Museum in Ft. Pierce, Florida. Please learn about this wonderful museum, all run by active and former SEALs and their friends and families, and who rely on public support, not that of the U.S. Government.

www.navysealmuseum.org

IF YOU GOT ANY CLOSER, YOU WOULD HAVE TO ENLIST

I also support Wounded Warriors, who tirelessly bring together the warrior as well as the family members who are just learning to deal with their soldier's condition and have nowhere to turn. It is a long path to becoming well, but I've seen first-hand what this organization does for its warriors and the families who love them. Please give what your heart tells you is right. If you cannot give, volunteer at one of the many service centers all over the United States. Get involved. Do something meaningful for someone who gave so much of themselves, to families who have paid the price for your freedom. You'll find a family there unlike any other on the planet.

www.woundedwarriorproject.org

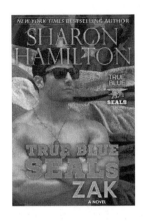

Video trailer for Zak:

https://youtu.be/WCvkz10Zczo

CHAPTER 1

Z AK STOPPED BY the Rusty Scupper, the SEAL watering hole in San Diego before leaving for San Diego International Airport to pick up Amy. He'd gotten up early since he'd been tossing all night long. Nerves. Not battle nerves, but those of the female kind. Bugged him that the training hadn't worked all that out of him.

This was going to be an important first meeting between Amy and his SEAL Team 3 buds. Sure, Amy had agreed to marry him, after a wonderful half-day of sex together. It was easy to make a commitment then. But would she still say yes after she really knew what she was getting into?

He wanted everything to go off without a hitch. Needed her first impression of his Team and their community to be perfect so she'd still agree to his plan. They had intended to wait until he got back from deployment before scheduling this meet and greet.

Zak's anxiety whispered that leaving Amy behind in San Francisco, where they'd foiled a terrorist attack, was unsafe. He hoped to convince her to move down to his apartment *now*, rather than wait. Then they could plan the wedding and get married when he came back.

He asked advice from several other SEALs while they waited for their food. He knew right away it was a mistake to do so.

"Get her drunk. That always eases things along a bit," said Alex.

"Don't fuckin' pay any attention to him. He's divorced and never gonna find anyone who will put up with him," said Calvin "Coop" Cooper. The tall surfer-looking dude, one of the Team medics and gadget guru, had an unflappable demeanor.

"You charm her," said Fredo, wiggling his unibrow up and down. "Ladies like to do romantic things. Walk on the beach at midnight, go for a swim. Right, Coop?"

Cooper grunted in the middle of a blush.

"Take her to a Padres game, man." Carter demonstrated a slow swing. "Ladies love baseball."

Fredo objected. "You livin' in some kinda alternate reality, Carter? That's just what you tell yourself. Nothing romantic about watching your lady ogling guys in tight, butt-fitting pants who make millions of dollars while you sittin' there in the sun with mustard all over your chin. You like that shit?"

"Works for me," returned Carter.

"Which is why you're still single."

Coop was still laughing at Fredo's comment.

"I'm just trying out the merchandise, making sure I gets it right," shrugged Carter. "And for the record, if she doesn't like baseball, well, that's a game-stopper for sure."

Zak knew there wouldn't be any baseball games due to his lack of funds. Walks on the beach were sounding better and better.

Carter stood, fist-bumped his friend, and left. Fredo, Coop, and several others said their goodbyes and wished him luck.

Lucas, Rory, and T.J. got up to leave, as well. Lucas added his two cents. "Some never like it here, especially if they're the jealous type, so be prepared. Or they like it at first, and then they turn on you so fast—"

"Hell, Lucas, you know better than to tell this young froglet that," said T.J.

Rory Kennedy leaned into Zak and winked, whispering, "Don't listen to any of them. Let the ladies convince her. She'll not believe anything any of us will tell her, anyhow. But the *girls*, they are great at answering questions and helping her out. They've been there and had to wrap their minds around the way we are. They have to like all their business known by everyone else, not having much of a life outside the community.

Some resent it. You're bringing her to the Barbeque at Coop's?"

"Planning on it."

"You're good to go, then." The scruffy-haired explosives expert scratched his Brillo pad reddish brown pelt and cracked his neck as he walked away, a slight limp in his gait, following behind T.J. and Lucas.

Zak steadied his breathing and then took off for the airport.

While driving, he wondered what Amy's reaction would be to the rest of the team and their wives. Deployment was in less than a month, since they were tasked with a short special TDI in North Africa. Normally, they'd be working up for several months, so this was very short, especially for Zak and Carter, who had to learn everything. Everyone else had been on their "off" rotation for nearly three months and had deployed more than once with the team on prior missions.

They were a well-oiled machine as a group, and now that he'd spent some time with them, he could spot other Special Forces or Team guys on the street. Everyone had a nickname that the ladies would probably think was belittling. Smack talk was the usual form of conversation. Hot buttons were discovered and pressed often for the good of the man, as well as the team.

He followed the turnoff to the airport.

As a sniper, he'd trained with Armando Guzman, the legendary shooter on SEAL Team 3. The man had more kills than the rest of the squad combined. Zak had been nervous at first, working so closely beside Armando, but that was nothing compared to the case of nerves he was sporting right now.

After parking the car, he dodged traffic at the arrival terminal and made it up the stairs from the baggage claim area where he could watch arrivals. He was still a half-hour early.

At first, he sat and watched people. Couples kissed, kids hugged their grandparents, and old friends shook hands and slapped each other's backs. A group of older women with leathery tans laughed so loud they drowned out all the other noises of the busy airport. The matching carryon bags identified them as Mexican Cruise ship returnees.

Zak got up to get a cup of coffee but wanted a beer instead. He went for a mineral water and couldn't decide if he was hungry or thirsty. His palms sweated.

He caught a reflection of himself in the mirror behind the counter, and it gave him a start. He'd gotten a bruise under his right eye from one of the fifty cals they'd been training with when it swung loose and caught him before he could duck. It was not unlike the way he'd last seen Amy. They'd survived that bombing at the MegaOne complex in San Francisco, and when he'd left her to join his team back in San Diego, they both had bruises and scrapes, as if they'd gotten into an altercation between themselves.

This bruise hurt so badly he was sure he'd gotten a hairline fracture to his cheekbone. He refused all x-rays, not wanting to risk a chance he'd be rolled back to stay home and heal. He was not a complainer and kept his mouth shut.

Zak's heart pounded, and his fingers began to tingle at the sight of Amy smiling down at the floor and weaving in and around the crowd, nearly skipping. Her stretchy dress had just the right amount of cleavage showing. The fabric hugged her awesome derriere and swung around her smooth tanned legs, peeking above her knees for some dangerous views of her thighs. The airport noise was muted, since he was on the other side of the Plexiglas barrier, so he watched in near silence until he realized he was holding his breath. He waved and then tapped on the divider. She looked up.

Her warm brown eyes sparkled as her face bloomed for him. He watched her breath hitch, stopping just long enough for him to see her distracted happiness. Then she hoisted up her shoulder bag and began to jog towards the exit. In seconds, she was in his arms, charming him with her lovely scent and filling his heart with joy.

He brushed aside her hair and kissed her neck first, whispering in her ear, "Missed you, sweetheart. I might never let you go."

She dropped her bag, stepped in to her tip-toes, rested her forearms on his shoulders, and framed his face between her soft lavender-scented palms, being careful of his cheekbone bruise. "Don't. Tie me up and use me day and night. Capture me. Don't let me go home. Nothing would make me happier!"

Being careful not to cave into the urge to slip his palms up under her skirt and feel her butt cheeks, he grabbed her rear and pulled her into him. At last, their lips mated. All his apprehension melted, and the entire airport vanished as his body awakened fully to her presence.

Her cheeks glowed when they came up for air as her eyes took in all of him, a mixture of wickedness blended with the good girl he knew she was at heart.

"Boy, have I had some dreams along that line, Amy. I'll admit. It feels like I've been on a fast."

She returned his chuckle. "I hope so."

"No worries here. You're the only one I dream about, sweetheart. I'll sign that in blood."

"I haven't slept for a week thinking about coming up here. I don't remember my dreams, but they woke me up lots of times." She purred into his chest, "And I was kind of sweaty, too."

Amy's suitcase arrived at the baggage carousel. Zak was quick to pick it up, and they exited to the short-term parking.

"We've got a barbeque tomorrow over at Cooper's house. He's a helluva guy. I like him a lot. From Nebraska. He's one of our medics."

"I'm game."

"I kind of thought it would be a good chance for you to not only meet the other Team Guys, but their wives and some girlfriends. We don't bring casual dates to these gatherings. You'll meet some kids, too, if I know Coop and Libby."

"Sounds nice." She adjusted her seatbelt as they made their way to the frontage leading to the freeway. "So if the guys scare me, maybe the ladies will soften the blow?" Her smart comment was followed by a smile and that tilt of the head that drove him nuts.

"You catch on quick."

"I have a good teacher." She snuggled closer, the truck's bench seat being very accommodating.

"Sweetheart," he bent and said to the top of her head, "I've only just begun. And maybe you can teach me a few things, too."

She reached for his package and gave him a squeeze. "I like that we'll rediscover our bodies all over again. Hasn't been that long, but when you said starved, well, that's exactly how I feel, too."

Zak was seriously going to have a zipper malfunction. He squirmed and cleared his throat. Amy was right to read that as a sign he was turned on as hell, and though he had to drive, she began unbuttoning his flannel shirt. Her breathing was soft like butterfly wings on his neck—and then on his chest as she bent down, raised his tee shirt, and kissed his nipples, giving the left one a tug with her teeth. He focused on keeping his hands on the steering wheel, but it was damned hard.

"I'm right back at high school, honey, asking you to slow down. Except this time I know I'll have you all night—"

She cut him off with a kiss, her lips sucking his and inviting his tongue. "God, I missed you, Zak."

"Now I'm worried we won't make it home before—"

Her fingers had unbuttoned his jeans and slipped inside his shorts, finding him in the flesh and again giving him a nice squeeze.

"Holy shit, Amy, I don't need another accident. You know that, honey."

"Oh but, Zak, this is no accident." She fondled his balls. "So if you're that worried, why don't you take me some place private, okay?"

"I'm just getting used to the area, honey. Not sure where—"

"Behind a building. A parking lot not in front of a

ten-story building. A rest stop." She struggled to inhale and then moaned. "I'd fuck you"—she climbed on his thigh and rubbed herself against his tightened muscles, her knees squeezing the sides of his right leg— "anywhere. Even in a restroom or a storage closet. You get my meaning?"

Oh yes, he got her meaning. He just couldn't think at the moment because all the blood in his brain had traveled like the Pony Express down to his lap.

SAN DIEGO COUNTY was peppered with golf courses, but could he find one now? No! Their habit, started during their hot and steamy high school off-and-on-again trysts, was to do it on a course. It was so bad that every time he drove past a club and eyed the green manicured lawns, he got hard just thinking of Amy and all the times they'd urgently screwed. His boners interfered with practice rounds he attempted with some of the other SEALs.

At last he found something and hoped they had a quiet corner or convenient coat closet at the *Read and Feed* Bookstore, which was the first establishment he came across. He turned across another lane of traffic, causing cars to honk in protest as he entered the parking lot. Amy slid off his lap and was adjusting her clothes, her palms smoothing down her chest as she perused him wickedly. It was so unfair.

Holy shit. We won't make it into the coffee house.

He buttoned his fly and his shirt, turning to her. "Best I can do, sweetheart. We'll be creative. You up for this?"

"No worries, cowboy. I'm ready, as you can see." She held up her panties.

THE SCREECH OF espresso and smooth jazz playing in the background did little to calm his nerves. He scanned the combination bookstore and coffee house, which was dotted with solitary and pairs of readers of all ages, sitting at clusters of square tables with mismatched chairs. A backdrop of bright artwork adorned the brick walls. None of the rapt readers paid any attention when Zak and Amy arrived.

The barista had earplugs that nearly touched her shoulders. Her well-muscled arms were covered in colorful ink.

It was reflex that pulled Zak to the counter, turning at the last minute to Amy. "What can I get you?"

She tipped her head back, gazed at the chalkboard menu, and pressed her body against Zak's entire backside. She was making sure the bone between her legs rubbed against one of Zak's butt checks with a wicked right and left movement. Her hands started at his hips and slowly slid down underneath the tops of his jeans, an action the barista raised her eyebrows over.

The feel and vibration of her voice next to his ear triggered a tingle down his spine, ending in his crotch. "I'll have a peppermint mocha. Room for cream." Her low sultry whisper was barely audible.

"Coming right up." The lady didn't even ask Zak what he wanted.

I'm getting everything I wanted, and then some.

Zak drew an arm around Amy's waist as she nibbled on his earlobe. "I hope she's fast. I like fast, Zak. You need to be inside me fast."

He was blushing—and very grateful no one he knew was in the café. Her words warmed and sparked him all over, the tingling traveling over his skin like a tiny electric current.

"Patience, my love. They say it's a virtue," he said between two short kisses.

"Not when you want to be fucked," she whispered back.

"Amy, I'm yours just as soon as—"

"Here you go, Miss." The barista sounded like a snake with her "s" sounds. The afterthought of Zak's needs dawned on her. "Will there be anything else?" Her eyes lidded over, and a crease formed on the right side of her mouth.

Zak ignored her and laid a five-dollar bill on the counter. His gesture was returned with a look that made him feel like road kill.

"You can keep the change."

"Yes." There were those snaky sounds again.

Maybe she has a forked tongue, too.

Amy leaned in front of him, giving his inner elbow a good feel of her ample breast. Her little mewling sound was a nice touch, followed by her picking up the cup and putting it to her lips. Her brown eyes focused dead center to Zak's, and she slurped the whipped cream, leaving a tiny moustache. The challenge to do something extraordinarily stupid was laid down. Zak fingered her cream moustache and put it in his mouth. "Amy, come on back here," he said as he led her away from the counter. "I have something to show you."

Of course, Amy would stare down at his bulging groin area. The barista abruptly turned.

Inserting a finger in his belt loop, Amy took the lead, pulling him behind her as she wandered in search of a place they could be more intimate.

They found a purple velvet oversized chair in the back corner. Zak slid it discretely to the left so the main café area couldn't see it. She pushed him onto the cushions as his hands reached for the nude lips of her sex, feeling her pulsing wetness. He turned her around and guided her down on his quickly unsheathed cock.

His upward thrust reminded him of their chemistry, the hot hormones of their young love mixed with something he now knew as a full grown adult man he never wanted to be without.

It was a far cry from a golf course, but as he felt her grind down on him, giving him full access to her warm wet channel, his hands overflowing with the warm pillows of flesh her breasts made, he observed where they'd wound up. Directly in front of him was the sports section. At eye level were big books. One in the center read "The World's Most Outstanding Golf Courses."

He smiled. Some things never changed.

CHAPTER 2

T HE EXCITING ENCOUNTER with Zak left her wanting more as soon as it was over. The forbidden public sex and her nerves all added to bring her to a crescendo and an orgasm that was still racking her body long after he'd finished.

She rocked back and forth on him.

"Baby, that was awesome," he said, kissing that part of her neck that sent chills down her spine.

She kept her eyes closed and focused on every movement his cock made against her tingling insides. She dug her nails into his thighs, still feeling the long rolling spasms that would not release her. Grateful, she secretly hoped it would continue all night long.

"Someone's coming, sweetheart," he whispered. She heard the polite coughing as if someone wanted access to the row they were occupying.

"I can't," she said, unmoved. "Oh God, Zak, I can't stop."

His warm chuckle did little to cool her passion. "Baby, I love that about you."

"I could go forever."

"I know you could," he said to the back of her neck, his fingers squeezing her tits, pinching her.

She continued to rock against him. His inhale told her if they were in bed he'd be ready to go again almost immediately. She heard the clearing of a throat behind them. "I don't care. He can watch," she gasped.

Zak urgently put his fingers under her dress, and as she rocked him, he massaged her little bud, which helped her come to the full climax and then start to retreat down the other side.

"God, baby, thank you," was all she could think to say.

"Thank *you*," Zak whispered.

She glanced over her shoulder. A handsome older gentleman was smiling, but not looking directly at her. Zak's fingers slid down her thigh, his chest leaning forward against her, spreading her skirt over his lap while he buttoned his fly. "Is there someone there?"

"Yes, Zak. He's waiting."

"Fuck."

She couldn't remember seeing him blush before, but it definitely was a blush on his cheeks as they repositioned the chair and made their way, hand in hand up front, without checking back to view their intruder.

Without her panties, Amy reveled in the feeling of the moistness between her legs and hoped it would be a permanent condition for the very brief visit of only three days.

"That was a first," Zak mumbled as he opened the door for her.

"Me, too. But it was wonderful." She kissed him, resting her wrists on his shoulders. Zak's palms naturally smoothed up her thighs.

"So we're so very hot tonight, then? I guess you're not hungry? I was going to take you out."

"Well, you did take the edge off a little. A small salad would be nice, Zak." She *was* starved, after all. Recalling the morning getting ready and then flying, she realized she hadn't eaten anything but a banana since breakfast. She regretted leaving the rest of the hot creamy mocha on the floor by the chair.

Zak picked up her panties and held them down at her feet so she could put her red toes through them and slide them up to her hips.

"Thank you. I like how you do that," she said.

"I like how you do that, too, sweetheart."

She forgot that in the evenings the San Diego area had a gentle breeze, and his arm around her shoulder softened her chill, as he pulled her hip against his. The small Italian restaurant was open for lunch, but sparsely populated. They took a booth, sliding over the smooth oxblood red leather.

Zak appeared healthy, tanned, and stronger than she'd ever seen him. He'd always been in great physical shape. With all the soccer and football and other sports in high school, he was the one most others were compared to. But today, seeing the size of his arms, which had gotten huge, the thick chest muscles connected to more muscles extending up his neck, his square jaw, and the way he honestly returned her gaze without flinching or diverting away showed he'd grown up years just in the few weeks they'd been apart. He was an enhanced version of his former self, and that former self had been pretty damned good, too.

He laughed at her after they'd ordered. "You keep staring at me like I'm going to jump out and spook you or something. What gives, Amy?"

She'd never noticed how white or straight his teeth appeared, how smooth his lips were, or how when he swallowed he used more muscles than she'd ever seen. He'd always been the best looking guy in high school, heck, in the whole town. But now, his handsomeness was focused, sharp, and well-honed.

His palms were a bit callused, the right side graced with one new scar. Corded veins roped up his biceps and down his forearms. Even his fingers were thicker. She wondered…

"It's just that you're different somehow. Bigger." She felt the flush of her cheeks and the light veil of sweat at her upper chest. An evening with him alone – all night long – was making her knees weak. She'd never seen him so magnetic. Just being anywhere near him always engulfed her in the flames of great fantasies, but today, she found an even stronger attraction, almost like an animal chemistry that wasn't present before.

"Bigger?" Now it was his time to blush. He cocked his head and winked at her. "So what you're saying is all the running on the beach, the midnight swims, and double PT is making me a little more…" He chuckled, and Amy's spine shivered. That dimple at the right side of his lips was getting deeper the more he smiled. When he let the smile bloom, when he opened his lips and gave her the full-on beaming face, she nearly fainted.

Yes, I've studied your body for years, Zak. And yes, holy cow, you've gotten bigger. You're stronger. You're just— She didn't have the words to describe her jumbled belly, the reaction her body had to not only the sight of him, but the scent of him as well.

A wine glass was dropped in the far corner, and instantly, Zak turned his head. His relaxed demeanor didn't hide the fact that he had taken in the whole room and everything inside it. The hairs at the back of her neck began to rise.

"Should I be worried, Zak?"

He scowled. "No."

She waited for him to explain.

"It's the training, Amy. I think my reaction times are quicker. Everything is quicker—" Catching himself before she could say anything, he continued, "Well, we'll see on that other thing." His smile wiped her mind of anything except the vision of them tossing in the bed together for thirty-six precious hours non-stop. He looked at her directly, eyes unflinching, not hiding any of his new intensity.

She sat back and let him see she was noticing how different he was. "Don't get me wrong, Zak. I like what I see."

As the waitress presented their food, Zak peered around her, raising his eyebrows. "I certainly hope so. Wouldn't want you to be disappointed, now." He wiggled his eyebrows again. "Would we?"

"You know I wouldn't. You're just—you're just different. More you. More of you to love, and I certainly don't mean you got fat. I loved the Zak I said goodbye to in San Francisco. But this one—" She opened her palms. "I wasn't prepared for what a change all this training was going to have on you. I mean, you're harder, but in a kind of gentle way." She knew she wasn't making much sense so scrunched up her eyebrows to ask for help.

Zak was playing with her, barely looking at her, a sexy smile gracing his lips as he toyed with his spaghetti, twirling it around the fork until he put a forkful of the delicious pasta in his mouth. His lips were covered with buttery Bolognese sauce. He raised his left eyebrow as he licked the substance with his tongue. Then he winked at her.

She was done. Frozen in place, just watching him eat. It gave her chills observing his swallow. His Adam's apple did the slow dance down and then back up again as he silently finished the whole plate of pasta in sheer minutes.

When the emotional fog lifted, she began to pick through her salad. She wasn't hungry all of a sudden. She felt his eyes on her and loved the feeling.

"Tomorrow, I can't wait to introduce you to the Team, especially my LPO."

"Leading—?"

"Leading Petty Officer. He's in charge of our little company. He's not a Naval Academy grad, but came up through the ranks like I hope to do some day. Kyle's a good man and one of the best I could serve under."

"Okay." She stared down at her salad and wasn't rewarded with any hunger pangs. She gulped down some ice water, chewing several pieces of ice. Zak again gave her that knowing smile.

"Now what?" she asked.

He shook his head. He grabbed her hands in his

callused palms. "Amy, it's just me. Just you and me, sweetheart. Why are you so skittish?"

"Nervous?" She didn't know what else to say. Words were completely failing her. "I don't know. It's like we're together for the first time all over again."

His thumbs caressed her knuckles and the backs of her hands.

She continued, "After all the times we've—"

"Fucked."

She tried to hide her shock. He brought her palm to his lips and kissed her tenderly.

"Yes, well, not like we aren't familiar with each other. I mean—" The hole she was digging was getting deeper, and Zak was enjoying it way too much.

He squeezed her hands, laying them back on the table. In a whisper, he answered the question she'd not asked. "Maybe because this time it means something. This time you're here to see if this is a life you could live. Amy, I want you to be a part of my life, this community. You have to be completely honest with me, because, honey, I'm done looking. I need you here by my side, but only if you can see yourself doing this. And if you can't—" Zak leaned back in the seat and dropped his gaze to the table then gave her that piercing stare that told her he was one hundred percent serious. "If you can't, we have to walk away. I need to deploy knowing you'll be good when I'm gone."

CHAPTER 3

A MY WAS EASY to love, insatiable in bed, and incredibly lusty out of bed; he was in a constant state of arousal. Since he no longer drank, taking her to one of the clubs—even if he had the energy to go dancing, and he doubted that right now—was not an option. Several of the guys had taken him to a western brew house, and he'd felt out of place learning the line dancing, but he'd try that with Amy. And he knew she'd like it.

Bars and even brew joints with dancing were for picking up girls. It was great for the single guys. But Zak, just like he'd told her, was done looking.

She snuggled into his chest, tucked in sweetly like she always did. Most of their trysts were done on a blanket at a park or golf course, so he was enjoying the luxuriousness of the king-sized bed and the smell of her body on his sheets. He decided he'd not wash them for a week or more, just to remind himself of these nights.

This trip was way too short, of course. There would, hopefully, be a lot of loving. But there was also a lot he had to accomplish, and he wondered if he wasn't trying to do too much too soon in their relationship. Reluctantly, he put that aside. Using his training to focus in on the task, he set up the plan and rehearsed it over and over again in his own head. Then he was going balls to the wall to execute. His hope was that it would be so well thought out, so well executed that she'd find it natural and easy to go along with everything he'd worked out.

Amy moaned, wrapping her legs around his thighs. He could feel the smooth flesh of her sex against him. Even in sleep, she was fully available to him and he loved that about her.

Zak's hands smoothed up and down her upper arm as he stared at the ceiling. He'd made the first step to do something important with his life by becoming a Navy SEAL. The Brotherhood was his new family and it healed and filled so many holes in his soul. Serving with men who would gladly die for him without thinking about it felt honorable. It was indeed what made him one of the lucky ones.

Now, Zak was about to do the next big thing in his life. He was "securing the target," bringing Amy into his life, not just as a girlfriend but also as a mate and life partner. He had been completely honest with her. If she couldn't take the intensity of his family now, couldn't deal with the stress and loss and tears and, the joy of doing something more important than all of them that sometimes came with the job, he'd have to walk away.

And as hard as it would be, he'd do it. He'd make sure he didn't give up on his shot to become one of the best of the best and to serve his country proudly with honor.

THEY WERE TO meet Carter at an omelet house for breakfast. He and Amy noodled around in the shower until they were going to be unfashionably late. He was always the one to have to turn down the heat so they could keep to a schedule. Amy would have been fine just staying in bed the whole time.

She made a point of showing him she wasn't going to wear panties, "just in case."

"This is going to be a painful day for me, I can see."

"I have the cure for that pain," she whispered.

"Indeed, you do." Her hopeful face was seeking out a message he wasn't going to give her. "You're here to learn about my community. And before you tell me you learned all you need to know in that bed," he pointed to the tussled sheets behind him, "I need to show you things. Things that are important for you to know. I'm doing this for you, Amy." He added a smile he'd almost forgotten to show.

She got that little stubborn teenager look as she continued dressing and then, examining the floor, turned her head from side to side, the pouty smile on her face. It enchanted him, but also reminded him that he really wasn't in control.

"Zak, I hope you're not tired of me already," she whispered to her bright red toes.

"Not a chance, sweetheart." He grabbed her and held her tight, tilting her chin with two fingers. "Stay just the way you are. Insatiable." He kissed her. "Sexy as hell." He kissed her again. "Riding my cock all night long like last night. I'm going to be ruined when you have to go back."

"Then keep me here."

Her clear brown eyes were honest, unflinching. He knew she was ready to take that step through the doorway with him. As long as everything else worked out over these next two days, he'd be able to convince her to get married before he deployed. That was the new mission. He didn't want to wait until he got home. There was a new target to be acquired.

CARTER HAD ALREADY had breakfast when they arrived. He stood, giving Zak an annoyed sneer before he even looked at Amy.

"You know, I'm sitting here, eating my eggs and

bacon, and thinking—no, I'm *knowin'*—what Zak's doing right now. And I'm sitting here eating cornbread and drinking more coffee than I usually do, all by my lonesome. I coulda slept in, man."

Carter's eyes darted to Amy and got round.

"Carter, this is Amy."

"Nice to meet you," she said and extended her hand.

"Oh, honey, we don't shake here. We hug."

Before either he or Amy could react, Carter had pulled her chest into his and gave her a big squeeze.

"Um. Nice. Very nice." Carter winked at Zak as he let Amy escape. With his fingers stroking his chin, he added, "Didn't he teach you that? That boy is not doing his job. Now, if you wants pointers and instructions, I'm your man."

Zak punched him in the arm. "You asshole."

After they all took their seats, Carter again directed his conversation to Amy. "You see how he swears now? Occupational hazard, ain't it, Jell-O?"

Amy turned to face him. "Jell-O?"

Zak didn't like that one of his most painful nights was being relived. Amy's father, now the Santa Rosa Chief of Police, had him arrested for adding red Jell-O in the opposing high school's fountain. Some of the opposing football team's members caught Zak and handcuffed him naked to the school sign. He was left as a present for Officer Dobson, Amy's father.

That was his senior year, and Dobson forbade Amy from seeing Zak any longer, not that it made a bit of difference. It just meant they had to sneak around a bit, which actually made it more fun.

"I can't believe you told him that story, Zak."

All he could do was shrug.

"Okay, you love birds. I got things I got to do. I'm not excited about spending the next hour watching you two fuck with your food, you know what I mean?"

ZAK TOOK AMY on a tour of the beach area near the Hotel Del, walking her down to watch some of the new BUD/S recruits who were just beginning their painful journey to glory. The little rubber boats, manned by men in orange vests, came in from just beyond the breakers, sometimes overturning and sending everyone into the water. The boats were carefully lifted over the slippery, sharp rocks that were a break barrier. The boat had to be protected. Footing had to be secured or an ankle could be broken, or worse. Zak remembered how black and blue his shins had been after those days and how it took nearly six months to grow the hair back on the top of his head from carrying those boats overhead.

"You did this?" Amy asked.

"Every SEAL does this." Placing his arm around

her waist, he said, "You're only seeing the tame parts. Those midnight wet and sandys, linked arm in arm, in the surf. Those are some times you don't easily forget."

"I'll bet not many of you guys own rubber boats, either."

Zak had to laugh at that one. "You got that right. Took me six months before I could even look at one."

"Why do they have to yell at them so loud?"

"Trying to pick a scab, get under their skin. See how mentally tough they are. Lot of guys are strong enough physically. The mental side is the killer."

"Bet you had it all scoped out before you went. I can see you doing that."

Again, this was funny to Zak. "As a matter of fact, the ones who do that usually wash out the first week or two. I think there's such a thing as overtraining. Mental overtraining is the worst."

She turned in his arms. In the warm space between them, she asked, "Why?"

Zak pulled her hair back behind her ears and off her forehead. "Because, darlin', there always comes a low day. One of those days that you doubt yourself. You have to be able to hang on long enough to get yourself and your buddy clear. If you panic, you're dead. And you might kill someone else, too."

THE PARTY WAS in full swing when Zak and Amy

arrived. The light coral pink bungalow with red tiled roof had a small front yard bordered by wrought iron fencing. Several dogs were roaming the lawn area, overseen by a new guy Zak hadn't met.

"Zak Chambers," he said after he let himself into the yard behind Amy. "This here's my fiancé, Amy."

"Zak, yeah, heard about you. Jell-O. I'm Dan Welch. Just got back from language school." The guy's face was handsome, enhanced by white teeth and an affable smile. Zak had been worried about Amy getting jealous, but he was feeling a bit of the green monster himself.

"Nice to meet you, Amy."

"Language school, huh? That's cool." Zak squeezed Amy's shoulder. "This is Amy's first time at a gathering."

"Oh, they'll be gentle on you. Nice bunch of gals in there. Can't say much for the guys, though."

Music hit them as soon as they opened the heavy oak door. Coop was dancing wearing a pair of fins and snorkel facemask, a small red cape from a child's pajama set tied around his neck. The thing looked miniscule, like a napkin, hanging down the back of the six-foot-four SEAL medic. Coop's nearly white-haired son of about four had the rest of the pajama outfit on, plus red girl's rain boots.

"Hey, there she is!" Coop came over and shook

Amy's hand. His goggles were getting in the way so he flipped them up on his head. "I'm Coop. You must be Amy."

Zak could feel her grip onto his fingers like a vice. He knew she was nervous as hell, but she didn't cut and run. He introduced her to several others, including Libby Cooper, Christy Lansdowne, a very pregnant Gina, and Mia, Fredo's wife.

"Gina's a cop, honey. She's married to the sniper I'm training under, Armando."

"Understand your dad's Chief in Santa Rosa?" Gina asked.

"Yes. Due to retire soon, I hope."

"Oh God. Me, too, I hope," Gina said, placing her palm against her belly.

Mia leaned over and rubbed Gina's stomach. "For good luck." Her dazzling smile was model perfect. "Gina is my sister-in-law. Armando is my brother. Fredo and I are working on a baby."

Zak had heard some of the talk about Fredo and Mia trying to get pregnant and decided not to mention a thing about it.

Lucas came forward, holding his blonde daughter who was about the same age as Coop's boy. She was squirming, giving her daddy fits. "Welcome to our family, Amy. Don't listen to Zak here, because he lies through his teeth. You do know about the Thursday night coed strip poker sessions?"

The line was perfectly delivered, and as Amy stepped backward and blushed, Zak held her arms, bent down, and kissed her on the cheek. "You know that's not true."

Lucas' girlfriend suddenly appeared, reached over, and grabbed the preschooler. "Here, let me take Lindsay so you can be introduced properly." She smiled at Amy. "We'll talk later. I'm Marcy, and I sell real estate, too, but down here. Or at least I used to." She stepped away and began showing Lucas' daughter a toy, bouncing and almost dancing with the child.

"She's really good with her," said Lucas. "With both my kids." As he watched them, he turned and added, "Marcy and I are getting married, just as soon as my divorce is finaled."

Zak noticed Lucas appeared to be bashful about this. Zak didn't like the fact that the ugly D word had come up, but it was a reality that SEAL divorces were common. He felt Amy stiffen as he wrapped his arm tighter around her waist.

Zak caught the eye of a woman he knew from Sonoma County. Kelly Freeman had been married to his former soccer teammate, Joel. The young SEAL was severely injured in a firefight and came home nearly blind in one eye. Joel had worked very hard to be able to stay on the teams, taking sniper training and becoming the only SEAL who was reinstated after what should have been a career-ending injury. And then on his next deployment was killed in a roadside bomb attack.

Kelly was dragging someone Zak recognized as another SEAL from Team 3 behind her when she stepped up to him, wrapped her arms around him, and gave him a kiss on his cheek.

"Stan said you were on his team. I couldn't wait to see you again."

"Wow, Kelly." Zak momentarily was flooded with scenes from the funeral back home, Kelly's puffy eyes and tear-streaked cheeks. "You look amazing." He introduced her to Amy. "I'm not sure if you guys ever met, but you remember the guy—"

Before Zak could finish, Kelly interrupted him. "Stan and I are getting married next year, Zak." To her fiancé, she said, "He and Joel knew each other ever since they were kids."

"What a small world it is." Stan was a little stiff, but accepting.

"You know, Kelly, Joel is the reason I decided to become a SEAL?"

Kelly threw her head back and laughed. "You must not have talked to him after he lost his eye. He'd have discouraged you, Zak."

"Nope. Never got to talk to him. I'm so glad to see

you've found yourself another frog."

She rolled her eyes. "It was a hard time, for sure, but," she shrugged and continued, "the SEALs kind of rubbed off on me."

"Pleased to meet you, Amy," said Stan. The couple walked away in search of beers.

Scanning the crowd, Zak found Kyle crawling on the floor with several kids on his back, playing horse. He maneuvered both of them over to his LPO's side.

"Whoa, partners. I've gotta go two-legged for a bit. Hold that thought, and we'll get right back to it," Kyle said in an old crusty prospector voice. The sounds of disappointed children filled the room. He stood, sweating profusely and breathing heavily. "Whew. That's a workout. Especially now that some of the kids are getting pretty big."

"Kyle, this is—"

"Amy. Nice to meet you, Amy." Kyle extended his hand.

"Thanks. Zak has told me how pleased he is to serve on your team." Amy was polite and sounded at ease.

"We do this about once a month when we're home. The ladies do this often so the kids can grow up together and play—in some cases, learn to play nice." Kyle winked at her. "My son, Brandon, is driving my wife nuts, and he's the one we have to watch out for."

"Probably in the genes." Amy's comment drew pink to her cheeks. She let off a nervous laugh as Kyle and Zak exchanged a knowing smile.

"Wouldn't be the first time I've heard it," answered Kyle.

All of a sudden, they heard someone yelling in a high-pitched, shrill voice. Zak's reflex made him check his right side for a sidearm, and he cursed himself silently.

The dancing stopped. Even the kids stopped playing and watched as a blonde lady nearly ran into Marcy, snatching the white-haired youngster from Marcy's arms, setting her down. Her own arms were full with a squirmy toddler who was terrified. "You get your filthy hands off my daughter. You stole my husband. Now you want to take my kids, too? You bitch!"

Lucas positioned himself in front of Marcy for protection and leaned forward to soothe his daughter, who began to cry. A couple of the other guys fanned out behind the woman Zak assumed was Connie Shipley, Lucas' soon-to-be-ex-wife. The toddler in Connie's arms reached painfully for Lucas.

"Connie. Don't start with this. You're scaring the kids." He tried to take the boy in his arms, but she turned aside. Lindsay continued to try to get to her dad.

"You bring them here to meet your fuckbunny?"

Several of the wives started to say something, but thought better of it. The men were casual, but it was clear to Zak if any harm was to come to the kids, his buddies would intervene. Connie was so insanely angry she appeared to be on drugs.

Each time Lindsay tried to go to her daddy, Connie yanked her arm back, a defiant look on her once beautiful face. Marcy retreated to the background, obviously opting to not further inflame the situation.

"Connie, you get out of this house or I'll call the cops. You weren't invited. Nobody wants you here. Get your shit together or I'll stop trying to be reasonable and fight you with every fiber of my being. You have no right to endanger my kids. You leave them both here with me." Zak had only known Lucas for a few weeks, but he'd never seen the man angry. Today, he was nearly bursting veins in his neck.

"Oh, isn't that sweet!" Connie sneered at some of the other SEAL wives. "You little trash-talking bitches. Pretending to be my friends. How many of you screwed my husband, too?"

Kyle came up behind Connie, peeled the toddler from her arms, and handed him to Lucas. "Ma'am, you're gonna leave right now or I will personally see to it that you are arrested. You've made your point. Now leave."

Connie temporarily lost her grip on Lindsay, who ran to Lucas. The youngster buried her head in Lucas' leg, hiding her face and her tears from her mother.

Zak heard a low level muttering of expletives from men and women alike as Connie was firmly escorted outside. Kyle and several of the Team guys stayed outside with her and did not return.

Amy wasn't moving. Her palm was to her mouth. She was shaking.

Of all the fuckin' parties for Connie to show up…

Again, Amy stiffened as Zak attempted to rub the back of her neck. "It's okay, sweetheart. Sorry you had to see that."

He tucked his thumb and forefinger under her chin, but Amy pulled away.

"I'm not a child, Zak. This isn't a divorce. The woman is unhinged and shouldn't be anywhere near those kids."

"Don't think you'd get an argument from anyone here. This has been a long time coming, apparently." He tried to wrap her in his arms, but again, Amy pushed him away gently.

"I'm okay, Zak. Don't do this."

"What?"

"Shield me. Smother me. I'm a big girl."

"I just wanted to—"

He was grateful she nearly whispered her reply.

"You can't take the ugly out of this situation. It's sad, really sad. But please, don't rob me of my feelings. There's nothing you can do to take it all away. Let me process it."

Kyle and several others didn't come back to the party right away. The dancing had stopped, although the kids began their play again. Lindsay jumped into the little circle of SEAL kids. Lucas hung onto his son, discussing something in private with Marcy.

The women were in clusters, whispering and searching the front door for further news. At last, the crowd saw flashing lights as the police took Connie away in a patrol car. Even from inside the house, they could hear her protestations and filthy insults.

The party didn't end anything like Zak had imagined or envisioned. He decided to give Amy the space she seemed to need and resigned himself to just wait until she wanted to talk. Whatever questions she had, he hoped he had answers for.

CHAPTER 4

THE RIDE HOME was difficult. Amy kept searching for meaning in her jumbled stomach. The drama was painful. And it also brought back memories of the last time she felt agitated. It was during the attack at the complex in San Francisco where she worked. Perhaps what bothered her most was that Connie was part of the community.

"You know them very well, Zak?" she finally asked.

Zak had also been quiet, passively watching the road as they made their way back to his apartment. She knew he was filled with things he would never mention to her, and she was bothered by it.

"I don't know many of them well. Carter and I have been through all the pre-workup at Great Lakes and then the BUD/S training. Lucas and the rest of the guys, even Kyle, I'm just getting to know." He didn't look at her when he asked his follow-up question. "Why?"

"I was wondering if she had some mental illness. Or has she always been like this?"

"I have no f—idea, Amy. This was the first time I've met her. But there have been stories."

"I'll bet."

They drove in silence for a few minutes longer, peeling off the freeway and coming to the network of narrow streets winding up to the apartment complex. Amy wanted to ask questions, but felt Zak would be critical. She bit her lower lip, took in a deep breath, and let it out.

"That bad, huh?" he said to her.

"No. Just not what I expected."

"So what did you expect?"

"I don't know. Does this sort of thing happen a lot? All this drama? Wives marry other SEALs? Wives go ballistic?"

"Come here." Zak reached over and pulled her beside him. He gave her shoulder a squeeze and then gently gave her a one-handed shoulder massage. "You have to understand something. There's always drama. Just never comes out that way. I've talked about it with some of the Team guys. It isn't all hearts and flowers, Amy. I mean—"

Zak paused, stopped caressing her shoulder and upper arm, and patted her instead.

"Usually the drama surrounds some guys, like Joel,

who get injured or never come back. That's when the community closes ranks, comes together, and helps the spouse and family. It's just what they do. And I'll be honest and tell you, some guys, when they go overseas, are unfaithful. There can be drama there, too. The ladies stay close to home, form this network of strength. They usually can dig it out of anyone if something's going on. There aren't too many secrets. All the joys and pains are shared communally."

"Okay. I can see that."

"But as for Connie, I think she's just a mental case. Maybe she was, maybe she wasn't like this when they first got together, but she did demand Lucas leave the teams, and he's not ready to."

"That happens a lot, too? Wives beg their husbands to get off the Teams?"

"I don't know. Not been around it enough to really know. That's why I wanted you to come down here to meet everyone, to talk to whomever you wanted to talk to, answer all your questions. I want you walking into this thing with your eyes wide open."

"I think I do a pretty good job of that."

He glanced at her face. "You do, honey. I think you have great instincts. You're good under pressure. Remember, I've seen that."

How could she forget the look on the terrorist's face when his bloody handprint was left on the glass door of her office or later when she thought her life would end in that bomb blast?

But there was one lingering question she had to ask. "So, Zak, how often do SEALs get divorced? Is it a chronic problem?"

"What do you think?" Zak had pulled into the parking garage. Shutting the Hummer off, he turned in his seat to face her again. He focused on her hands folded neatly in her lap and gently covered them with his. His warm fingers wrapping around hers was comforting. She could see he was trying to formulate words for something difficult to say. He perused her chest, up her neck, and then met her face to face. "I think the statistic is better than sixty percent. That's all military, too. Maybe the SEALs are a little higher, but I'm not sure."

She broke eye contact and stared at the walls of the garage, swallowing hard.

"Thing is, Amy, it's hard on the families when the guys go overseas. That stress takes several forms. I guess Connie went on a spending bender, and then they had money problems. I just think she was weak and decided she couldn't handle it. We all wish she could have just been honest about that—she wasn't made for this life. No harm in that. But the way she's going about it is all wrong."

"Terrible for the kids."

"Tears Lucas up. It really does."

"I won't lie to you, Zak. I really don't know how I'll feel when you go overseas."

"I know that. That's being honest."

"But I want to support you. I know this was what you were made to do."

"That's absolutely for certain. But I want to make one thing perfectly clear. My dedication to this job will always come first as long as I am a SEAL. If that changes, then I get out. You need to know that."

It was one of the things that scared her the most. No matter how much he loved her, being a SEAL would always come first.

"And?" Amy knew there was something more he was leaving out.

"Let's go inside." He took her hand. She slid off the seat into his arms, and they walked hand in hand up to the elevator and to his apartment beyond.

He directed her to sit on the couch while he brought in some mineral water for both of them. Instead of taking his place beside her, he knelt in front of her. "Amy Dobson, you know me. You don't know the community yet, but I do, and I think there is a place here for you. I've got the green light from your dad."

Amy's expression must have registered shock because Zak hurriedly explained how he'd called Chief

Allister Dobson and her father had given him his approval.

"Kind of old fashioned, but I wanted to do it that way. I knew what your father thought was important to you, Amy."

The tender expression on Zak's face left her speechless. He'd planned this ahead of time. This was more than a just meet and greet with the other members of his SEAL Team; this was a planned course of action. Very intentional. She saw for the first time how he'd bared his soul to her. He'd set all this up.

"Marry me, Amy. You already said yes, but I wanted you to know that your dad is in agreement." He took her hands in his. "I want to make it formal. I don't want to wait for some day."

She didn't have to think about it. She went to bed every night and woke up every morning envisioning being his wife, sharing a life with this man. "Of course, just like I said before, I'll marry you, Zak. And in time, I'll learn how to support you the way I need to. I think I'm good with it all."

Her smile would usually bring a kiss, but he was still hesitating.

"What is it?" Now she was getting worried.

"I want us to get married before I deploy."

"Like when?"

"Soon. How about next weekend?"

CHAPTER 5

INTO THE NIGHT, they planned a small civil ceremony, followed by reservations at the Hotel Del Coronado. He knew she felt rushed, and he wasn't totally comfortable with it, either. It wasn't the ceremony that bothered him, but the two-day honeymoon. And that was squeezing a day out of their training just three days before they got on the plane. Kyle asked him if he'd be more settled with the quickie wedding and honeymoon.

"Yessir," was the only answer Zak could think to give him back. He was grateful for the extra day and night.

After it was all arranged and Amy flew home to gather her things and get the move scheduled, Armando was sporting a grin Zak wanted to wipe off his face. It was the best shit-eating grin he'd ever seen.

"What's the rush, Jell-O?" the handsome Puerto Rican SEAL asked. The two of them had developed a bond through their love of guns and special gadgets. Zak was easing into feeling a full-fledged member of his new team, and Armando was the ticket to get there.

"No rush. I just want it settled."

"Ah. So you're worried she'll change her mind after you go? You tying down all the loose ends, my friend?"

He'd asked himself the same question over and over again. Had he decided to do this because he didn't want to lose her or because he wanted his mind to be at ease when he was gone?

"Armani, I'm just ready, is all. I think she is, too." He adjusted his duty bag higher on his shoulder. They'd been participating in long-range target practice. "I want my bite out of the apple. Things happen. I know that."

"Yeah, but don't go thinking about it none. Remember, things happen, but not to you. You and I," Armani said as he pointed to Zak first and then to his own chest, "we come home. Just like all the rest of Kyle's squad."

AMY HAD JUST four days to pack up and drive to San Diego. Her replacement at the Omni helped her in the evenings, so they got it done in three. The last night, Cheryl stayed over. The apartment was going to be sold after new paint and carpeting was installed. Sales were slower, even though the summertime tourist season was well upon them. The number of second home buyers willing to pay several million dollars for a one-bedroom place, even in San Francisco, had dwindled, along with fears about the economy in the Bay Area. It didn't help that the terrorist bombing and shootout at Ferry Plaza had dominated the news for nearly a month. It was also something they had to disclose to a prospective buyer, due to California law.

She would miss the view of the Bay Bridge lit up at night, the ever-changing colors of blue water on the bay. Amy felt like she'd barely gotten to know her new digs. And now she was leaving.

But there was blue water calling her down in Coronado, too, and a life with a man who would probably never be able to afford such a place, but who was all she needed.

In San Diego, the planning had been so quick, and with their limited funds, the choices were slim. The wedding would take place in Cooper's in-laws' backyard, where several of the other SEALs had gotten married, as well. Libby's parents wanted to pay for the flowers and wine. With the kegs barely ordered in time and thanks to the other SEAL wives, everyone was bringing something for the wedding feast afterwards. It was going to resemble a common backyard summertime barbeque. She bought a dress that didn't need alteration from a local bridal outlet. Though it was last year's fashion, Amy doubted anyone would be able to tell.

As she loaded up the last of her things, she was suddenly anxious to be on her way and couldn't wait to start her new life. Far from feeling rushed, she urgently wanted to get back down to Zak.

Cheryl gave her a hug. "I hope everything works out for you, Amy. Although all this was fast, you've known Zak for years."

"We kind of grew up together."

"I'm grateful for the job, too. I'll keep in touch, and not to worry, if any of your past customers come back, I'll make it right with you."

"Thanks, but that's not likely to happen. Not like I was here very long."

"Well, you'll have a lot of other things on your mind. I can't wait to come visit you later in the year. Maybe keep you company when Zak's overseas?"

"That sounds nice."

"When is your dad coming?"

"He's flying down tomorrow with Marlene and Margrit. Love to be a fly on the wall for that conversation."

"Oh?"

"Margrit works for my dad at the station. She isn't always very discrete, so I'm sure I'll get an earful."

"Surprised he didn't want to drive you down there

himself."

"Oh, he tried. I just wanted this time to be by my-self, take this big step on my own." She remembered his answer when she verified he'd agreed to Zak's proposal.

'Amy, he's a different man now. He's ready to pro-tect you. I see that in him. I'm glad you're going down there to be with him. Get away from all this—danger.'

SHE NEVER STOPPED thinking about this important step in her life during her drive south. She thought about it as she watched him move her things inside his apart-ment. The bachelor pad became a shared space. There was evidence of her there: her favorite teapot, her coffee maker, her favorite sheets, and soap for the shower. She stood her toothbrush next to his and discovered they had the same brand. She hung her dresses in the space he'd left for her in the closet. Her wedding gown was already hanging in the corner of the room on a special stand.

As she added her things to his, she began to relax. She touched his razor and the special shave cream he used – all things she'd smelled and touched before, but that all seemed like a long time ago. Her world was blending with his. He found her smoothing over his shirts in his underwear drawer, inhaling his aftershave, rubbing the cotton fabric against her cheek.

His stealthy body moved behind her to spoon into her backside.

"You okay, Amy?"

She smiled and realized she'd been crying as tears spilled over her lower lids. "Never better. I don't know why these things move me so much. Just simple things, but they are the things you use every day. The things you hold in your fingers, things you've chosen. Like me. Like you chose me."

Perhaps I'm being silly. Overly emotional. Maybe that's not what he wants to see.

He lifted and parted her hair at the back of her neck, deliberately giving her a moist, passionate, and lingering kiss that made her spine tingle.

"I've been waiting for you to come into my life, Amy."

She turned. His eyes were watery, as well. Her thumbs caressed his cheekbones as she studied the unwavering gaze and the power of his breath on her face. "You chose me, Zak. You reached out and grabbed me. I will belong to you now."

"We chose each other a long time ago, Amy. But tomorrow it will be official."

She stood in the safety of his embrace, reveling in the warmth that was their shared love. For this space and time, life was perfect in every way possible.

IT WAS A Cinderella moment for Amy. Bright sunlight woke her. The cream-color sheets barely covered her naked body. Lying on her back, one arm draped over her forehead, she heard birds outside.

Am I dreaming? Have I died and gone to Heaven?

A massive shadow crossed her flesh, and then a divot appeared in the mattress as Zak sat next to her. His now-familiar after-shave enveloped her. She inhaled and allowed it to arouse her, heard the tinkling of the water left dripping in the tiled shower. A callused palm slipped under her sheets and moved slowly up her torso as she arched back, stretched but did not open her eyes. His fingers squeezed her left breast and then traveled to outline the smile that had separated her lips. She heard him lick his and swallow before she felt his flesh against her own.

The command was deep, needy, and yet protective. The fire in her belly flamed as her arms accepted the press of his torso against her. The anticipation of their lovemaking was driving her wild. Her arms were as needy as his, holding her shaking body against him, her thighs separating and rubbing against the outsides of his. He kissed her closed lids, asking her to see him.

"Zak." She wanted to say more, but was without words.

"Your day, Amy," he whispered between kisses. Into the hollow of her neck and then up to her ear, he sent his trembling voice. "Your day to be worshiped."

Their eyes found each other, locked, and connected. Zak's body slid over and between her legs, all the while not taking his gaze from hers. Their hands mated, outstretched and to the side. With commanding gentleness, he pulled them above her head, fastening them in place with one hand at her wrists. His other hand lovingly lifted her left butt cheek, angling her pelvis up to meet his hips. She raised her knees to accept him. Her need intensified as he entered her slowly at first and then deep, pulling out to plunge in again.

Amy's head arched back, and Zak placed a wreath of wet kisses under her chin, from one ear to the other. His relentless movements in and out, strong and steady, began a powerful crescendo, turning her insides to fire. He both coaxed and demanded she submit to his powerful body, yet brought her to such heights her self-control disappeared. She met his strength with her own powerful need to match his. Their lovemaking became a delicious shared mixture of dominance and submission, roles reversed and lovingly expressed back again.

In the bright sunlight, with the friction of flesh against flesh, he fed her with his kisses, not releasing her body until every quiver and shake was squeezed from her body. As birds twittered in a distracted afternoon sky, her mind traveling somewhere off to a distant future, she knew she would always belong to him. She knew the more he gave, the more she would need him.

THE CHAIRS WERE arranged with a nosegay at the end of the four rows on both sides. She watched as more chairs were added to the little ceremony. Zak was standing next to the chaplain, who had married several of the SEALs. Her husband-to-be's face beamed when he saw her.

Libby had given her the veil she wore when she married Coop. Amy wore the wedding pearls her mother had left her. Carter gave her an admiring perusal and a kiss on her cheek.

"Lovely, Amy. You are the perfect bride."

Margrit gave her a kiss, handed her the colorful bouquet of lilies and red and white roses, then turned to take her walk down the aisle on Carter's arm. A lute player began while Carter and Margrit took their places alongside the chaplain and Zak.

As the lute player began the stanza that was her cue, her father put his arm around her waist. "My little girl getting married," he said to the top of her head with a crack to his wavery voice. "I've thought about this day, and you are even more beautiful than I imagined. More beautiful than your mother the day I married her." He kissed her through the veil. She cast her eyes downward so he didn't see she noticed his tears.

She knew it was a special day, made even more special by the fact that there might be many more or only a precious few of these days to celebrate. The world was a dangerous place and the SEALs did dangerous things. Time would tell. So she took it all in, enjoying what she could, knowing no one could predict the future.

The path she took down the brick patio to the man who waited there was a smooth one today. She would draw strength from it now as she knew some day she'd need that reserve. There would be worry while he was deployed. Looking into the faces and bowed heads of the women in the audience, she vowed to rely on their collective unwavering grit and to give back what she could to this little community of warriors and the people who loved them. She wasn't just marrying this man; she was marrying everything he stood for, his way of life, and the ethos he carried. That honor and ethos had chosen him, not the other way around. She prayed it would choose her in time, as well.

As she got close to Zak, she said a little mental prayer to herself, while feeling the heat from his body the closer she got to him.

She wished she could make these next two days

something they'd never forget, never regret, and something worthy of reliving forever.

The words were spoken. Her father kissed her cheek again, handing Zak her left hand, and then took his seat in the front row next to Marlene.

"Forever, Amy. No matter what," he whispered. The chaplain's words were nearly drowned out. "This is forever. I promise I will always come back to you."

A shiver traveled down her backside when he said those words. She composed herself, licked her lips, and whispered back, "And I'll always be waiting for you. Your home is in my heart."

He squeezed her hand, brought it to his mouth, and kissed it.

CHAPTER 6

Z AK WAS STILL buzzing with the visions of the two days of lovemaking they'd had, even though he was rocking inside a loud transport plane. He was glad the beast was so loud. He didn't want to talk to anyone, since it gave him a few hours to get lost in the memory of her sweetness.

Every time he closed his eyes, he saw her body in front of him, how she felt against him, as she rode him, as she begged him to urgently take her, begged him to be gentle. If it hadn't been for the mission, he'd have stayed in bed with her for much longer.

They'd eked every minute they could out of their last night together, so he also realized some of this was the fog of lack of sleep. The other men seemed to sense it and left him alone. Carter kept up with the Cheshire cat grins, though Zak pretended he'd not seen them.

Their plane landed, sounding like it had burst a tire on impact. He left his earphones on the longest of anyone, struggling to say goodbye to the images and dream state he'd been immersed in. Hearing the high-pitched whine of the engines and feeling the furnace-like blast from the dry Moroccan air brought his daydreams abruptly to an end. The team began moving immediately, not leaving any time to wallow in a second good-bye, even if it was a virtual one.

"We're to meet the Secretary at the hangar," Kyle barked over the sounds of equipment and the engines. As soon as it was unloaded, the big transport would be taking off for another location. Part of the plan was to not draw too much attention to each other.

Zak scanned the airspace after seeing Kyle do so. Since there wasn't anything else on the field that looked big enough to take the team and their equipment, he figured another plane was due in soon.

He followed T.J. inside the hangar. At first, he couldn't see a darned thing. It was as hot as Hades, despite the low light. The moving van-sized fans did little to cool anything down.

Their group was stopped at a desk and, one-by-one, had to give up their side arms. Since Kyle and Armando didn't raise an eyebrow to this, Zak cooperated. His Sig Sauer was checked and disarmed by a guy with arms the size of Zak's thighs, who slid a tag to Zak.

"Last name only."

Zak watched Armando fill his out after asking about his KA-BAR, and the specialist gave him the non-verbal horizontal all clear.

By the time he passed through the gauntlet of the entry guards, his eyes had primed to the darkness.

Zak had never seen anyone who had been on national news before in person, but United States Secretary of State Porter Harrison was leaning over maps on a large conference table, being briefed by an unidentified security detail. He looked up long enough to register he didn't know anyone in Zak's crowd and then went back to focusing on the table. Everyone was wearing Kevlar except the Secretary. A tall aid, heavily armed, standing off to the side sprouted a grin and came over to Kyle. The backslapping made enough noise that it caught the Secretary's attention, a worried frown and lined brow showing up on his graying face. He straightened up and called to his man.

"Lyman, what gives?"

"Sorry, sir. This is my old LPO, Kyle Lansdowne. We go back a bit."

"That so?" The Secretary placed his fingers on his slim hips and adroitly slipped around the table to stand in front of the two men. He searched Kyle's face briefly before he extended his hand. "Porter Harrison. I've heard about your squad, Lansdowne."

"Thank you, sir." After checking the grin on

Lyman's face, he added, "Or at least I hope it was good."

"Oh, it was good, all right. You guys took out that cell in Tennessee and put us on the trail of another one in San Diego. Non-sanctioned, of course, but we liked that. Saved the Bureau a lot of time."

Zak was hoping the "we" was the Secretary and the President.

The rest of the squad stood behind Kyle in a semi-circle. Force of habit made them fan out to watch the communication between the Secretary and their LPO.

Kyle turned slightly. "Lyman here was our medic for a time. Coop transferred over from the East Coast when Lyman retired."

"Never got the pleasure, man," Coop said as he shook the former medic's hand.

"Well, he's still not retired," the Secretary chimed in. "Part of my security detail. But you guys are gonna make it unlikely I'll need his expertise, right?"

No one said a word. Zak had lots of questions. Although he was preoccupied during his flight over, he figured no one else had been told much about the mission, either.

Lyman cleared his throat. "I think a short briefing, sir, since the bird isn't here."

Harrison squinted and added a nod. "We're waiting on the private jet to get us to the Canaries. Owned by the same man who's lending us the villa."

Zak knew several of his buddies felt naked without their pieces. The lack of information forthcoming was making some of them nervous as hell. And now they were meeting in a villa on an island? Zak had thought they were conducting something special in Casablanca or Marrakesh.

The Secretary scanned their group. "I'm meeting with an old friend from Stanford, Youssef Amir. Believe it or not, we both were recruited to play soccer."

A polite ripple spread through the crowd.

"Amir's father was a visiting engineering professor at Stanford, same department as my father, so we met when he was about ten and came over with his parents and two sisters. They even stayed with us for a couple of months before their living arrangements were made. We played on the same traveling teams growing up— all through middle school and later college prep academy. Then we both got recruited and admitted to Stanford. I was one of only two U.S.-born soccer players on the team."

Secretary Harrison was caught in deep thought for a minute, as if the answers to the mysteries of life were embedded in the concrete floor under his feet.

Kyle just stood and watched the Secretary until he continued. They could hear a plane overhead.

"The United States is opening negotiations with Amir, who is positioned to become the next Prime Minister here in Morocco, to see if our goals are aligned." He scraped an imaginary mark on the concrete floor. "For obvious reasons, mostly relating to his own personal health, we want those negotiations to be conducted in secret. So we've picked a villa in the Canaries owned by an English billionaire."

Kyle had cocked his head to the side and was watching the metal roll up door rattling in the desert wind. Then he glanced over to Lyman, almost as a challenge to the man. It telegraphed how little Kyle liked the situation they were getting into.

Harrison's attention angled up to the ceiling, hearing the plane. "I think our ride is here. Let me give you a brief rundown of what we're doing. As of the time we leave this hangar, you will be playing the part of bodyguards to the Secretary of State, who is having an old rendezvous with his friend, a little R&R. We want it to appear to be a vacation, not an official state visit. Just something low key, hobnobbing with the rich and famous."

The team grumbled.

"We want reasonable deniability that you are not SEALs or attached to any branch of government. You are bodyguards for Amir and me, hired private contractors."

"As in non-Government sanctioned job?" asked Coop.

"Yup. That's about it," answered Harrison.

"Who knows about us?" Kyle asked. He bypassed Porter and stared directly at Lyman.

"No one. Everyone who knows about you is back in D.C."

"So where's our backup?" Coop asked.

"You're looking at it, gentlemen," said Lyman.

"Extraction?" Kyle asked, drilling into his friend.

"If need be, we have naval maneuvers at Kenitra Airport, a joint exercise with the Moroccan air force. That's been scheduled for months, so we thought this would make good cover. We have a ship arriving tomorrow morning as part of that operation. A small combat force is embedded on the base, EET, Emergency Extraction Team among them. After World War II, the base was used as a Space Shuttle alternative landing and tracking site. We're pretending to upgrade tracking equipment we'll be sharing with the international community, but it's been fully controlled by the Moroccans since 1988. They have allowed us to use it for the Shuttle and Space Station programs as recently as 2005. But, gents, it's five hundred and ninety miles away, and it's only as a last resort."

"So, gents, that's it. We don't speak of this any longer outside this hangar. That's the game we're playing here," said Lyman, bringing his hands together and giving a dismissive clap.

Zak thought the gesture was more like a washing of hands.

The Secretary and all but three of his security team departed through the hangar door one by one. Harrison carried a rucksack. The plans that had been spread over the table were rolled up and sticking out of the side, as if he were a hiker marking trails.

"The guy's not even wearing protection," Zak whispered to Carter.

"Fuckin' makes no sense. Even a businessman would wear Kevlar."

"I don't think Kyle likes it, either," Zak answered.

"Shh." Fredo had his finger to his lips. "We are not alone here. Watch your mouths, froglets."

Kyle wasn't as worried about letting non-Team guys know his feelings toward the mission. "Lyman, there's no air support, no backup really. The Secretary isn't even wearing a vest for Christsakes."

"I know. That's the way he wants it."

"Is he all there? You think maybe he's sucking on someone else's Kool-Aid?"

The President had been known to have strong feelings about the use of diplomacy almost to the exclusion of a show of force. And he'd been controlling wars from behind his desk in D.C. rather than allowing the commanders in the field to call the actions. The feeling was strong that the military was having to win wars with their hands tied behind their backs and then was harshly reprimanded for losing those battles.

"Nah, Kyle. I think this is all Porter's idea."

"Okay, get your gear and follow them out," barked Kyle. To Lyman, he added, "I want a one on one with him as soon as you can arrange it safely."

"Look, I'm familiar with these kinds of missions. Did these all over Europe last year."

"Europe is not fuckin' Morocco."

Lyman watched the men pick up their gear and head for the door, being led by the rest of his detail. He lowered his voice, but the echo chamber of the hangar made it so Zak and Carter could hear him perfectly. "He might be stupid, Kyle, but Porter's a decent guy."

"Decent guys get shot, Lyman. You of all people should know that."

"Roger that, Kyle, but he's on a mission, and this is his friend. He thinks a heavy military presence will endanger Amir."

"And what about the Secretary?" Kyle asked.

"I don't think he's even considered that. I'm supposed to keep him alive until December, when the guy's retiring and going back to Virginia to be a law professor."

"Unbelievable," muttered Kyle. "He should have never left Virginia."

CHAPTER 7

AMY HAD LUNCH with Christy Lansdowne and a couple of the other SEAL wives. Gina was in her modified uniform, her white smock covering her very pregnant belly. She looked like she was headed for work afterwards. Marcy and Libby were dressed casually. Christy wore a suit, her briefcase and cell phone not far away.

"I'll take you over to the office tomorrow, if you want, and introduce you to my broker," said Christy.

"Thanks, Christy. To be honest, I was going to ask that very thing today." Amy had been wondering if it was too soon to approach the beautiful wife of her husband's squad leader. She noticed Marcy was smiling at the two of them.

Gina's phone pinged, and she texted something back to the sender, waiting for a response.

"Well, you can always go to my former broker's office. They do have a vacancy. Course, if you drop my name, you'll get booted right out of there." Marcy held her hands up in the air before Christy could object. "Just being perfectly honest. You know how the boys like their honesty!"

"We're gonna fix that, Marcy. No reason why you can't do real estate here in San Diego," said Christy. She turned to Amy. "Marcy had the unfortunate experience of trying to represent Connie—you remember her from the party—and Lucas with the sale of their home."

"But I thought Marcy and Lucas were…" Amy stopped, not wanting to step on any toes. Christy was mum.

Libby scrunched her face. "You brought it up, Marcy. You get to finish. Let's see how you can talk your way out of this one."

Amy was thoroughly confused.

"I'm just going to tell her the truth, ladies, okay?"

Gina crossed her legs, shaking her head. Libby sat back with her eyebrows raised. Christy didn't look pleased. "You have to now," muttered Gina.

Marcy adjusted her body on the metal chair, turning to address Amy, just as the waitress brought their lunches. She watched the presentation of food until the waitress left. She cleared her throat, leaning in. Amy matched her body language and bent forward.

"Lucas and I met and got together when I was hired

to sell their home. I knew better. I just couldn't help it. That's the God's truth."

"It's caused a lot of problems, as you observed during our barbeque," added Libby.

Amy felt a twinge of regret that Zak hadn't totally leveled with her. "I wasn't told. It still doesn't excuse Connie's behavior. I'm sorry, Marcy. It must be hard for you."

"One of the things you learn, Amy, is that things happen at very inopportune times. They deploy right in the middle of stuff. We try to hold off on big decisions until Kyle's home, but the rest of the world doesn't always cooperate," said Christy.

"Arguments. We're careful about stressing each other out before he leaves." Libby Cooper's work as a marriage counselor was showing. "I'm on pins and needles, making sure I show how proud I am of him, reassuring him I've got everything under control with the house and the kids, so he doesn't have to worry about me. We talk when we can during deployments. But you know it isn't the same."

Amy addressed Marcy again. "So you have a mess on your hands until he gets back. That what you're saying?"

"You could say that. No time for a court ordered custody arrangement, but part of her release from jail was predicated on her cooperation, given that Lucas had no one else but me to help with the kids. Not the best situation, but we're dealing with it."

"Marcy's got her hands full," sighed Gina. "Look, I'm going to have to run."

"Get it to go, Gina," said Christy.

"I got a couple bites. No worries. We have something we're working on, and I need to be there." Gina started to pull a twenty-dollar bill out of her purse, and Christy stopped her.

"Don't be ridiculous. Go. You want me to drop it by the station?"

"No. Not going there right now. Take it home for later, okay?" She gave Amy's shoulder a squeeze as she stood up. "Sorry I couldn't stay longer, but you got my number, right? Call me and we'll go do something. I'm going on maternity leave starting next week."

"Thanks." Amy watched as the very pregnant policewoman tried, with some difficulty, to weave in and around lunch tables, until she broke free at the street and disappeared.

"In case you're wondering, babies are born when they're overseas, too. We try to time it, but that doesn't always happen," whispered Christy.

Amy was grateful for the life lessons. "I suppose it took all of you awhile to feel totally comfortable with all of this. I've only had the shortened crash course."

"That's all most of us get, Amy," said Libby.

She looked between Marcy and Libby. "I guess you've both got your hands full."

"Libby's mom is babysitting all four of them this afternoon to give us a breather. She loves it. We're going furniture shopping after lunch. You should come with us."

"Maybe I will. Thanks." Her mind turned to the situation with Marcy and Connie. "So what do you do if there're more problems with Connie?"

Marcy sighed. "Unfortunately, most of that has to be handled by my attorney, which costs money. That's the real problem. But at least the attorneys talk, so I don't have to get that involved. I do all the dropping off and picking up, and so far, so good."

"Must be hard to get a sitter, someone you trust."

Christy sat up straight. "Never use a sitter. We have a babysitting pool. No one but relatives and other Team families have anything to do with our kids."

"Sort of our code of conduct," added Libby.

"We work together on the home front, just like the guys do overseas," said Christy. "Some deployments are easy, some complicated. We knew about Lucas and Connie splitting up. But they'd been fighting for months." She studied Marcy's face before proceeding. "We all knew Lucas did his best. But then he moved into the Bachelor Pad, and they didn't help him at all."

"Have you guys seen that place?" asked Marcy.

Libby and Christy shook their heads. "Imagine really raunchy posters and no housekeeper. They live on fast food, car shows, alcohol, and video games."

Amy's cell phone rang. Her father's number flashed on the screen.

"Amy? This is Marlene." Her voice was breathy, like she'd been running.

"What's wrong?"

"It's your dad, I'm afraid. He's had a massive heart attack."

This can't be happening!

"Is he—is he okay?"

"Not really, Amy. He's alive. I think you better try to fly up. I'd like you here when they complete the workup on him. He's stable for now, but on monitors. They warned me it's highly likely he'll have another one soon. I'm not allowed to see him, of course. The doctor is giving me only limited information."

"I see. I'll catch something right away and take the bus up from the airport, I guess."

"I'd come down to pick you up, but I don't want to leave him, in case…" Marlene began to sob. "I'm so sorry to have to call you while your Zak is away. He was feeling so good. We got back from San Diego. He was happy, excited for you and your new life."

"Maybe it was the flying."

"Listen, we can talk later. You need to get to the

airport. I'll call you if anything further develops. Text me your arrival. Let me see if I can get someone to pick you up at SFO. I just called the station, and the guys have been great."

Amy allowed the fear overtake her. There were two men she cared about in the world. One was in harm's way, and the other was lying in a hospital bed, perhaps near death.

Christy followed Amy to their apartment where she put together some clothes in a weekend bag. Kyle's wife was on the phone, checking for a reservation.

"Not having much luck. Why don't I just take you over to the field, and you can throw yourself on the employees. Southwest is probably your best bet."

In an hour, Amy was texting her arrival time to Marlene. If someone left Sonoma County, they'd just barely get there in time to meet the arrival.

OF COURSE IT would be Rich Wilson, one of her father's promising new recruits, the one who had taken her to a couple squad events. She never considered them a date, but today, she was grateful for his kindness.

His sad face told her he genuinely cared about her. She found it easy to walk into his arms and let out the tears she'd been holding back on the plane. Rich whispered things she couldn't hear, rubbed her back, and held her carefully. She appreciated the fact that, when she pulled back, he didn't cling.

"Come on. Let me have that," he said as he grabbed her bag. "We should get on the road. I brought the cruiser, so we can put on the siren."

"Does that mean I have to be the perp in the back seat?"

"Funny. You can sit up front or in the back. I'll be going so fast no one will see."

TRUE TO HIS word, they made it all the way to the hospital in less than forty-five minutes. Amy texted Christy to let her know she'd arrived and promised updates. She also let Marlene know when they crossed the Marin/Sonoma County border.

Any updates?

No new ones, which is the best news there is. We just hope this will continue.

Rich peered into the rear view mirror. "Any news?"

"Just that he's not had further attacks. I guess that's what they're worried about most."

"I thought the guy was strong as an ox. Has he been having any problems?"

"Not a one. Not that I know of. Dad is kind of secretive, you know."

"I hear you. That would be like him to hide something from everyone. God, I hope it's something they can regulate."

"Me, too."

Amy let the brown hills pull on her heartstrings as they zipped by. It was familiar, but everything about her world had changed in a flash of quick decisions. Coming back home didn't feel like it normally did. This used to be home. Used to be where she thought her future was. Now it was her past. She'd taken the big brass ring of a new life with her handsome SEAL, and now was being yanked back to the smallness of Sonoma County.

She wasn't a resident of San Diego long enough to feel like that was her home, yet. With her father in danger, her footing was unstable. She tried to think of something Zak could have said to her.

'Pay attention,' he'd say. *'Don't lose your focus. Think about your surroundings. Be vigilant.'*

But unlike the attack in San Francisco, this was a different kind of danger. This was something she was powerless to control.

'Then control what you can control,' she heard Zak advise in her mind. *'In a dangerous situation, don't panic. Panic is the enemy of solution.'*

What solution, Zak? Tell me. What am I supposed to do except wait for an outcome?

She leaned back in the seat, checking her phone screen. Should she text Zak or should she wait until she had more information. What would he want? He'd want all the information she had. Why bother him until she could give him a prognosis or an update.

Rich turned off the siren as they approached the downtown Santa Rosa outskirts. She watched his handsome profile and straight back, the way he carefully maneuvered the cruiser to an emergency parking space in front of the hospital entrance. She was overcome with gratitude.

He was outside the car in a flash, opening up the rear door, grabbing her hand, and taking her bag as they ran to the reception area.

"Allister Dobson. He was brought in with a heart attack. I'm his daughter."

The desk clerk gave them directions to the Cardiac Care Unit.

"Good news is, this one's the best in Northern California. They have all the best doctors and equipment."

They entered the double frosted glass doors. The sounds of monitors overshadowed everything else. In the small waiting room off to the left, they found Marlene.

The two women hugged. "Oh God. Thank God you got here."

Amy's fear was holding back her tears. She did not want to hear bad news. Until then, she'd buck up and think positive things.

"Has his doctor come by?"

"Just as you were leaving. He said they had run some tests, and the blood test confirms he did have a heart attack. They asked me about allergies."

"None that I know of."

"That's what I told them. He asked me if he took meds. And, well," Marlene blushed.

"He doesn't take anything I know about," said Amy, who realized Marlene had hidden something from her. "Marlene?"

"Viagra. He was taking a generic herbal Viagra, he said. Not the real stuff. It was from some pharmacy in Canada."

"What did the doctor say?"

"He asked me to go home and get it. He wants to see it."

Rich interrupted them. "Let me take you, Marlene. You shouldn't be driving right now. We can be right back."

Amy was again grateful for Rich's concern and for his help. "Thank you so much. I think that's a great idea. Marlene, why don't you go do that?"

After the two of them left, Amy broke down and let the tears pour out. She missed her dad, but she missed Zak, as well. Her mind scanned the scenario she was most horrified over.

What if I lose them both?

CHAPTER 8

THE VILLA COMPLEX consisted of thirty-five rooms—nine of them bedrooms, nine bathrooms, two kitchens in the main house, and a kitchenette in each of the two guesthouses. In addition, the main house was set up with offices a small off-shore corporation could be run from. The property was on the very top of the peak at Maspalomas on the main island with views of the bright turquoise blue bays and neighboring verdant islands sprinkled like pebbles in the Atlantic. A dusting of white sailboats and some large yachts littered the cays and bays in the area, where the rich and famous from Europe played.

Zak found a flier for the property with several pictures he'd want to show Amy when he got back, as well as the compound map and main house floor plan. Before anyone could notice, he slipped it folded into his vest and scanned the area to make sure no one had noticed. It struck him as odd he felt he had to sneak.

He began scanning the great room off the kitchen while the staff was making lunch. He was thinking about the things he'd read. The house was rented as part of an asset management firm's portfolio, but he noted none of the contact information was from the U.S. Most of the brochure descriptions were in Spanish or French. There was also a page attached in Chinese and another in Arabic.

He thought it odd the Secretary of State would choose this particular location for an important meeting, since he obviously was concerned for safety. Otherwise, he wouldn't have gotten the SEALs as part of his detail. He felt for his sidearm when he heard something that sounded like broken glass.

"Oh sorry!" One of the ladies fixing lunch for the Secretary had dropped a wine glass on the floor. "I pick it right up. No one walk here barefoot," she said in a British accent. She scurried away as two other women scolded her in a tongue Zak didn't recognize. Outside, a gardener was blowing leaves off an unused patio next to a deep blue lap pool.

Everything about the place had the look and feel of a billionaire's hideaway. The peaceful setting and bright colors were endearing. Yet something wrong. Zak was on edge, and he couldn't put his finger on why.

T.J. and Kyle were at the doorway. "Something

wrong?" his LPO asked.

"She just broke a glass is all," Zak told them.

Kyle peered over the countertop, as if checking on the array of fresh fruits, breads, and cheeses being lavishly spread out amongst flowers. Zak knew he was double-checking the source of the sound.

When he came back, Zak motioned Kyle follow him to the hallway study.

"We gonna be able to wear our sidearm soon, Kyle? I'm just not feeling very safe or secure here."

"His security detail has them. Remember? You're just a bodyguard, Zak." He must have delivered a disapproving glare because Kyle added, "You're hired meat, Zak. Quit looking so spooked. Only a SOF guy would feel that way."

"Not much good, are we then?" T.J. agreed. Zak was happy that his comments had found a friend.

"It's what the Secretary wants. When the staff leaves, I'll see if I can get the okay to carry. Until then, we go around armed to the teeth and the locals start asking questions."

It still didn't satisfy him.

They were in three man teams, taking turns, and always rotating at least one person to the next shift so they could pick up on something that didn't fit. Armando, Coop, and Carter accompanied the Secretary and his security chief, Lyman, down to the little village town to go shopping with one of the cooks. But they were made privy to the fact that Secretary Harrison needed to pick up a message left at one of the banks he was going to visit. He'd taken an empty valise.

Amir was to arrive tonight just in time for dinner. His plane would land in cover of early evening darkness, and he'd be driven up to the villa in a private limo.

Two other teams of SEALs were patrolling the several acre grounds, pretending to be guests, walking close to some of the workers to double check what work was actually being done, or sleeping on their off-shift in one of the guest houses. No one was without their phones. The use of Invisios was not allowed here, since they didn't want to appear like a paramilitary group.

Finally, they heard the Secretary's car rumble up the roadway from probably miles below. When Zak found the vehicle, he noted a small Jeep was following a good distance away. Relieved when the Jeep turned off onto a reddish dirt trail, Zak put it out of his mind and focused on the Secretary.

The driver of the car was wearing dark shades and bore no expression. Zak didn't like he couldn't see his eyes. The cook was animated as she attempted to bring in a package, which was quickly lifted and carried in by Carter and Armando instead. She made some comment to one of the girls in the kitchen, and Armando answered back in Spanish. The two helpers laughed and blushed in response. Zak could see Armando was quickly worming his way into their hearts.

"Armani is a babe machine, Kyle. He can charm anyone." Zak was laughing so hard he forgot he'd been previously on nervous alert.

"One of a kind. Think it works if he's seen as sort of a ladies' man. Doesn't seem to be affecting Mr. Friendly here, though." Kyle pointed to the stone-faced driver who abruptly turned the corner and went back to park the car.

"Only thing we still need, Lansdowne, is the ability to get firepower. I don't like that it's locked up in someone else's safe." Zak was as serious as a heart attack. "I'm naked without a gun. And I don't have the people skills Armando here has."

Kyle grabbed his shoulder. "You're a good man, Zak. You got talents. But I'm gonna see if we can get our guns back. I'm with you on that. I'm feeling exposed on all levels."

"Nothing defensible here."

Kyle nodded. "Point taken. Let's go see what the Secretary can give us."

Kyle asked for an audience and got it. Pat Lyman came with them to the study, closing the door behind. Zak and T.J. stayed to the corner while Kyle sat across the table from the Secretary of State.

"Mr. Secretary, I respect you as a great man doing wonderful things for our country. You are a warrior, sir, and I can see you are not easily intimidated."

"Why thank you, Lansdowne. I appreciate that." Porter Harrison was obviously flattered. Zak had been warned Kyle rarely bestowed such praise on anyone, unless he was after something in particular. T.J. crossed his arms and chewed on a toothpick, watching the two seated men.

"You got to understand, and Pat here can back me up, we come at these things from a totally different angle, sir. We don't suspect there's evil out there ready to kill us. We *know* there are sons of bitches out there ready to destroy everything we hold dear. To whom loss of life, even their own or their families and friends, means nothing. We are stronger than they are, sir."

Harrison nodded, but his lips formed a frown.

"You didn't bring us along to be human shields. We can't protect you unless we have access to our guns. Even if we can't wear them, we can disguise them somehow so it isn't obvious, even to a trained militant. But we can't even get our guns because they're locked up."

"I promised Amir the only people who would have guns are on my personal detail."

"So maybe Amir has a death wish. Maybe you do,

too. But we're tasked with protection. We can throw knives, win out in hand to hand combat, swing a baseball bat and crack someone's skull to protect you, but without the tools of our trade, we're nothing, sir."

"You're not nothing. You're also here to be my eyes and ears. To notice things."

Kyle shook his head, swearing to his feet. "Let me put it to you this way. You're a diplomat. You use words. Those are the tools of your trade."

Harrison nodded in agreement.

"I can see you're good at it. That's great. We need men like you."

Harrison again agreed.

"But that's not us. We blow shit up, pardon me, Mr. Secretary. We shoot people, and we shoot to kill. And we have thousands of hours of training to determine who the bad guys are and who the good guys are. Thousands of hours in the arena of war, where you have to make up your mind in a split second whether or not someone can be trusted. Even then, we make mistakes. Not many, sir. But if you insist on keeping our guns from us, well, you might as well ask us all to go home because I guarantee you we cannot protect you. And we'll all get killed if there's an event."

Harrison agreed with Kyle. Zak could see it in his eyes. But something else was going on.

"You don't understand, Lansdowne. I gave my

word. This man is risking his life coming here. I can't very well just tell him I changed my mind because some SEALs told me so. I don't know you, Lansdowne, but I trust you, and Pat here does, as well. Trusted you with his life, so I'd be stupid not to heed your warning. But I've known Amir for over twenty-five years. It took me nearly three years to convince him this was the right course to pursue."

It was Kyle's turn to nod. "I understand, sir." Resignation laced through his words.

"It will be the first thing I'll ask Amir when he arrives tonight. You have my word on that."

"Fair enough." Kyle stood, shook the Secretary's hand, slapped Pat on the arm, and motioned for the three SEALs to leave the room.

CHAPTER 9

A MY WAS ABLE to see her father before Marlene
returned with the bottle of herbal Viagra her dad
had been taking. His face was ashen. She didn't understand all the tubes and wires attached to him. One tube
went directly into his chest cavity. Sunken cheeks and
puffy, swollen fingers replaced his once rugged good
looks and healthy glow. There were more age spots on
the back of his hands than she remembered he had
before.

The man had always been her staunchest defender.
She used to think he could successfully duke it out with
any man who tried to defy him. The fact that Zak
always seemed to elude his long reach as the town
Chief of Police only used to make him angrier. And
now, finally, he'd given up protecting Amy, only after
being convinced someone else could do the job.

She knew he and Zak would have a long and very
powerful friendship as the years went by.

If I don't lose you, Dad. And then of course came that fear for Zak's safety.

Words the SEAL wives had given her earlier comforted her.

You'll never feel so loved.

They can't help it. They'll protect the innocent even if they have to sacrifice themselves in the process.

They are loyal to their wives and children.

It is a calling.

And then there was Zak's favorite: *'We're the ones who get 'er done and get out.'*

Allister Dobson stirred, groaned, and began to scratch at something on his chest. Amy could see he was trying to get to the heart pic.

"No, Dad. Don't touch that. You're in the hospital, and this is helping you get well." She gripped his hand, squeezed it, then leaned over to give him a kiss on the cheek.

Dobson opened his eyes, wide with alarm. His brow slowly furled, leaving a deep crease at the bridge of his nose. He didn't seem to recognize Amy at first, and then his expression relaxed. He even chanced a smile. "I was confused as to where I was. What hospital?"

"Memorial. The heart center."

"Oh, good." He scanned his private room. "Looks like some kind of command center. You could run a whole department with this much equipment."

Amy was glad his humor was returning and took it as a good sign. "No, Dad. They're just here to manage your little lonesome. All this is for you." After letting him get his bearings, she asked, "How do you feel?"

"Like a stuffed pig ready to be put on the barbeque. I got more meat tenderizer in me than the average Costco chicken."

"Have you seen your doctor?"

"No, why? Is she cute?"

Now Amy knew he would be okay. "I understand you've been taking some new medication."

"I only take blood pressure medication. I'm healthy as a horse."

"Which is why you're here."

"Maybe they need to take down the dosage. I got sleepy. Then I couldn't hold my eyes open, but my chest hurt like a son of a gun."

"Well, they've verified it was a heart attack. Officially. I'll wait for the doctor to come in and explain things, so I'll learn about your prognosis right alongside you."

"Where's Mel?"

"Marlene?" she asked.

"I call her Mel. It used to be my shit for memory, but it kinda stuck."

Amy laughed. It felt good to spar with her dad. She

valued each and every opportunity she had left. "Marlene went home with Rich to get some medication you were taking—*not* the blood pressure pills. Apparently something else." She pretended not to be paying attention to him, being more interested in the ceiling above his head. Dobson nearly blushed as recognition began to light up his face.

"Those are herbal supplements."

"And from what I've learned, dangerous when you're on blood pressure meds."

"Amy, I was—"

"No need to explain, Dad. Believe me, I understand. And I don't blame you, but apparently, a lot of people misunderstand their potency, and it can lead to serious complications."

Marlene flew into the doorway of the room, escorted by a nurse. "Ali? Can you authorize me to come in, please?"

Amy looked back at her dad, whose face lit up at the sight of Marlene. "Ali?"

"Her name for me. But don't tell anyone, please." He tried to right himself, but was still in the prone position, the tubing making traction difficult. "She's my girlfriend. Please let her in from now on."

"Only one at a time," the nurse said.

"I'll go outside and see if I can snag the doctor," said Amy. She closed the door to give them a moment's privacy.

DR. NIJJAR WAS reading the label on a bottle in his hands. She nearly ran into him as she exited her dad's room.

"I'm Amy Dobson, er, Chambers. I'm Allister Dobson's daughter.

"Very nice to meet you, Amy." They shook hands. He glanced down at the label again. "I think I have figured out the problem. Your father has been taking a generic Viagra that is interfering with his blood pressure medications. He must have been taking this without his physician's knowledge. This was a very bad thing to do."

"Is he going to be okay?"

"All indications are that what he suffered will leave some damage, but not critical. We will know more in twenty-four hours. His EKGs are returning to near normal again. We monitor other things, but it looks like he's headed in the right direction, provided he doesn't get stressed or move around too much. But there is no way to know exactly how much damage he's done to himself. Do you know how long he has been taking these?"

Amy was both relieved and concerned. She tried to recall the last few months. Her dad and Marlene had been dating about five months. She didn't think he had another "friend" so guessed she was the reason he wanted the Viagra. "I think only a few months, maybe five. He'll be honest if you ask him. No worries there."

"Okay, good. I'm going to have to speak to him. I want him to plan on retiring as soon as he can get his health back."

"Good luck with that."

"Yes, it is a frequent problem for many men. You want to join me then? I was just going to see him now."

"But the nurse said only one at a time, so she sent me out."

"Well, I'll make an exception. Let's go see him, shall we?"

Dr. Nijjar pushed the door open, and they found Marlene sitting on the edge of Allister Dobson's bed. She quickly stood.

"You're all right, ma'am. Just take a seat over here so I can look him over a bit." Nijjar motioned to a chair in the corner. Amy remained standing at her father's feet. "So, Chief Dobson, I have good news and bad news."

"Go ahead. I'm ready," Dobson said.

"The good news is that we've identified what could have triggered your heart attack." He hesitated. "And the blood test confirms it was a heart attack."

"The bad news?"

"We aren't sure how much damage was done. It's

way too soon to make any specific treatment plans. We'll have you here for several days while we evaluate your system and come up with something that will hopefully prolong your life." He held up the purple bottle. "But these will not be going home with you, and you should never take another one again. Do I make myself perfectly clear?"

Her dad's eyes locked with Marlene's. She gave him a warm smile and answered for him. "Of course. We'd rather have him alive as long as possible, doctor. That won't be a problem." Marlene scooted her chair closer to the bedside and took his hand, giving him a soft kiss. "You are so foolish, Ali. I feel like part of this is my fault."

"Okay, kids. Now I have to do my job. I'm sending you both outside while I take a good look at him. I'll be out shortly. Agreed?"

Amy and Marlene exited the room slowly. Marlene glanced back at her dad with a long, sober face. Amy could see she really loved her dad. Taking Marlene's hand, she led them to the little waiting room where Rich Wilson was still waiting.

"Oh my gosh, Rich. I didn't realize you were still here." Amy gave him a hug. "Thanks."

"How is he?"

"Well, he hasn't had another one, which is good. It's wait and see," Marlene offered. "Did he say when he could return to work?"

Amy didn't want to have the discussion about retirement in front of one of her father's men, so shook her head. "Sorry, no." She stepped closer to Rich, slipping her palm over his upper arm gently. "I'll have Marlene drop me off at Dad's house. I'll be fine. You should go. Let everyone know down at the station it appears he's out of danger for now, and we promise to keep them apprised, okay?"

Rich nodded, biting his lower lip. "You let me know if you need anything, Amy. Anything at all."

She watched his muscled form amble down the hallway. Rich was a good man and would make a caring and wonderful husband and father. As if he sensed she was watching him, he turned. His cute expression of surprise and crooked smile made her jump at being caught.

"Oh, by the way, congratulations. Happy for you, Amy."

"Thanks." It was all she could say. Her heart was missing Zak so bad. She needed his arms around her. She needed him telling her everything would be okay. She wanted to call him, but they had agreed to let him do the calling, due to the nature of the mission.

"Where is he, though?" Rich asked.

"Overseas. I think its North Africa."

He considered saying something. She could see it

in his profile. He finally gave her a good-bye smile and added, "Well, you need anything, I'm here. And thank him for his service, will you?"

"I will most certainly do that, Rich. Thank you for your help."

Amy and Marlene sat in the waiting alcove. The cardiac unit had no windows, but she knew it was way past sunset.

"Marlene? I think we wait until the doctor comes back, and then we both go home to get a good night's rest."

"That sounds like a plan. You want to get a late supper?"

"I'm just not hungry. I think I could sleep, though."

"Well, let's find out, and then we'll do that." Marlene took her hand in hers. "Thank you, Amy, for that wonderful weekend at your place in San Francisco and the shopping we did." Her grey eyes had tiny flecks of brown at the centers. "Thanks for allowing me to be part of your family. I know you must have feelings about your dad dating again after such a short period of time, but—"

"It's all right, Marlene. I want him to be happy. Everything about his house reminded him of my mother. That wasn't any way to live. He's a nicer person now, honest."

"You think so?"

"I think it's good for him to spend time with you."

"Really?" Marlene blushed, putting her hand over her mouth. "Oh. My. God. I had not hoped you'd feel this way. Thank you, Amy!"

"It's the truth. You're good for him. I want what's best for him."

"Well, thank you." She squeezed Amy's hand again.

Amy decided it was time to bring up what the doctor had told her. "Marlene, I think you should also plan that perhaps he'll be forced to retire."

"No! Really?"

"For my dad, that's going to be very difficult. It's way more than a job to him. It's a calling. Something that defines him. He sees our little city as the kingdom he's tasked with protecting. What does a man do when he can't do that anymore?"

"Very good question." Marlene was lost in thought. Amy could see she'd not considered this before. "I guess I was naïve to think he could go back to work. Did the doctor tell you this?"

"He suggested we consider it. I'm hoping he's talking to him now about it."

Just then Dr. Nijjar popped his head around the corner. "Ladies? He's all yours. And I've lifted the restriction on having two visitors. But don't stay long. We need to keep him quiet and rested. Nothing to upset him. No drama, please. Let's get through the next twenty-four hours and then make a plan for his healthy future."

"Sounds good to me. I think I'll just say good night and let him get some rest," said Amy.

"Me, too. I'm taking her home, so it will be a quick visit."

"Thank you, ladies. I'll have more information for you tomorrow."

CHAPTER 10

YOUSSEF AMIR WALKED into the villa like a king. His dark hair, greying at the temples, was professionally straightened and styled. His coffee brown skin was nearly as flawless as a woman's, though the man was almost forty years of age. He was fit and twenty years younger than his childhood friend, Secretary Harrison.

Zak noticed even his nails were buffed. He had an *en camera* appearance at all times, his head tilted back and peering out through half-lidded eyes. He held his driving gloves in one hand and slapped them nervously against the palm in his other. An attendant was parking his red Maserati.

"Porter!" he called out in his slight Moroccan accent. "Or should I call you Mr. Secretary?"

Zak saw his fluid movements beneath his cashmere sweater and dress slacks, which definitely seemed out of place on the island. Underneath it all, however, was the body of a fighter. He had the eyes of an eagle, all the while appearing casual and unconcerned. Zak guessed the man possessed a photographic memory and a keen intellect.

After they shook hands, Secretary Harrison addressed the SEALs present.

"These are my boys, Youssef. Highly trained. And just as you instructed, unarmed at the moment."

The comment seemed to delight Amir. "Very good." From a distance, he examined each of the men, one by one, thoroughly. "So you are the legendary U.S. Navy SEALs? What team are you and who is your team leader?"

Zak felt the sweat run down his spine. Kyle didn't move a muscle. Neither did Cooper or T.J., which told him they were on red alert to something that didn't add up. Even Lyman straightened up, adding a couple of inches onto his already considerable frame. He kept his focus on Amir, but Zak knew he was using his peripheral vision.

The Secretary's head whipped around in a movement that suggested he hadn't heard the man correctly the first time. He stuttered his words. "Youssef, I didn't mention these men were SEALs. They are part of our State Department private security detail." Harrison's calm demeanor was beginning to shatter. The look he gave Amir was almost a plea for mercy.

Amir gave a wide smile after eyeing the team again

one more time, slowly. To Harrison, he added too coolly, "I'm just making a little joke, Porter. No reason to be concerned." He walked to the Secretary and draped his arm around his shoulder. "Come. It has been too long since we sat and shared our pictures. It's time for a bit to eat and for two old friends to just be that, old friends."

Harrison found it inside himself to make a joke. "Watch it. Who's saying I'm old?"

Amir's laugh was hearty. Harrison's was a mere croak. Zak could tell he was not feeling comfortable.

"Sir, you want us all here, or are you going to be okay tonight?" asked Lyman.

"We'll be fine," Harrison answered.

"So I'll leave Coop here and Fredo. We'll retire to the perimeter for the night," said the former SEAL.

"Perfect."

The Secretary and Amir sat across from each other, the small square marble coffee table between them.

Kyle stepped forward and addressed Harrison. "Sir, we had a request of you, if you will remember. We'd like to address that request now, if you don't mind. Then we'll retire."

"Oh. Right. I promised." Porter scrunched up his face in a sour look. "My boys here would like you to reverse your prohibition on them carrying weapons. They feel they can better protect us—both of us,

Amir—if they are armed."

The Moroccan seemed to take forever to turn around to address Kyle, who had been standing at his back. "That's a fair question. I'm going to sleep on it tonight and will let you know in the morning." He turned back to the Secretary. "We got our guys watching the compound tonight, and they're very thorough. But tomorrow, the security will be on you, so perhaps that makes sense. But not for tonight. Tonight, no one knows I'm here or that we're meeting. Let's have a little pomegranate juice, some dates and figs, and some goat cheese. Get some rest. All of you."

The silence was awkward. Zak wondered why Harrison didn't protest this change in protocol. He knew why Kyle didn't say anything further. He was going to grill Lyman until he got satisfactory answers.

"Let me get them situated in their rooms, and then I'll return," said Pat Lyman. "I'll ask the cook to come in and serve you."

A full moon lit up the mountaintop, giving them good visibility along the stone pathway to the bungalows. The Secretary's other men were outside, walking the perimeter. The stars were bright, too, as if trying to outshine the moon. Carter had started to ask a question.

"Zip it," said Lyman in a terse whisper. He nodded to one of his detail, who was carrying an automatic weapon, pacing between the front entrance and the parking garage.

Lyman unlocked his bungalow, and all the SEALs threaded inside. A split second after Coop closed the door behind them, Kyle pulled Lyman up by his shirt collar, slamming him against the wall.

"Just what the fuck was that? I find out you had anything to do with any of those decisions about this fuckin' meeting, I'll see to it you spend the rest of your days so tied up with paperwork and government attorneys you'll wish you worked at Taco Hell."

Lyman was bigger than Kyle, but not by much. "I had nothing to do with it. I swear. This is all fucked up. I agree with you one hundred percent." Lyman pulled Kyle's arms down, readjusted his shirt, and walked to the bedroom.

"Hey, what the fuck?"

From the bedroom, they could hear Lyman say, "Fuck this. I'm getting you guys your sidearm."

"That's more like it," T.J. muttered under his breath.

Zak heard the heavy metal squeak of Lyman's gun safe opening. One by one, each man was handed their weapon back, along with extra clips.

"So far so good. Now you want to tell me how come the Secretary of the United States needs to meet with this asshole and wants to do it without proper protection or his security team even being armed?" asked Kyle.

"I'm as shocked as you are. Actually, I think the Secretary knows he screwed up. I'm guessing he wants me to give you these, just didn't want to say it in front of Amir."

"Lyman, aren't you tasked with keeping him safe? How can you do that when he's tying everyone's hands behind their back? He have some sort of death wish or something?"

"He's put a lot on the line. He's risking some political skin. But I agree; I've never seen him so unconcerned for his own safety. It's like he's willing to take risks he wouldn't have taken before."

"Who is this Amir fellow? Because, right now, he's not looking like a friend."

"Kyle, I'll tell you what I know, or what I've been told. The two of them were extremely close in their younger years and then rekindled their friendship as they both began their political careers. I think he's a friend all right. Lately, they've been corresponding with each other nearly daily. He told you their story. What he didn't tell you is something he brought to the security team. There's going to be a coup in Morocco. And this time, the king, the royal family might be vulnerable. The U.S. is informally charged with protecting the monarchy. But if the king goes, it could destabilize the whole region. Right now, the king picks the Prime Minister. If there were a coup, there might not be a Prime Minister."

"What's the uprising about?"

"Corruption, which is always a charge leveled. But there's help from the outside. I'm not sure who all the players are, but he wanted to get our foot in the door. He's using his friendship to forge a back door safety net alliance between Morocco and the U.S. Something that will hopefully protect our interests should a coup actually happen."

"For the purposes of what?" asked Kyle. "What do we need them for?"

"They have a fledgling tech industry here, sort of like a tiny silicon valley. Amir's family is involved in several electronics components companies—they make things for drones and satellites." Lyman had finished locking the safe. "And there is tons of equipment somewhere in Morocco. We'd like to help control a little bit where it's being sold off to. Someone is making big bucks doing that. We don't want it going into the wrong hands. You do remember Benghazi, right?"

"Holy shit," said Fredo.

"Look, I'm going to have to get back to him. I need to bring one of you with me. Your choice, Kyle."

"And if we're to get any sleep, I'd like to post three outside, to work alongside your guys."

Lyman agreed. "Pick who you want. Let's get going ASAP."

"Um, just so you know, I brought backup," T.J. said.

"I did, too. I got an AR-15," said Coop. "I can wear it so no one will know."

"Holy shit. Me, too. Brought my H&K," said Armando. Fredo indicated he'd brought some small explosive devices. A couple of the others confessed to bringing extra weapons as well.

Fredo produced several Invisios, letting Kyle hand them out. He gave one to Zak.

"You didn't really expect us to come unprepared?" Armando told Lyman, who had been standing with his hands on his hips. "We'd never do that. Neither would you."

"Understandable. I'm sort of glad you guys took that initiative to disobey," Lyman returned. "Hindsight and all, right?"

"I snuck in an extra Glock, but man, we were lucky we didn't have to fly commercial and go through customs," said Kyle. "You guys get your gear, and Fredo and Coop, you two will come with me and take the first shift outside. We spell each other every six hours, you copy?"

The team nodded.

"Zak, I'm sending you in here with Lyman. I want

you wearing Kevlar, but don't show your weapon. Everyone else, get your stuff together, but try to get some sleep. Armani, I want you to stay wired. Anything goes wrong, I want you guys in contact. I have a feeling it's going to be a long night."

T.J., Armando, and six others headed to the second bungalow while Kyle, Zak, Lyman, Fredo, and Coop moved toward the main house. Lyman introduced the SEALs to two former Rangers who were on his security detail.

"Come on. And don't show that Sig Sauer, okay?"

Zak showed him his ankle holster. He didn't tell him about the Ruger he had in his waistband.

Amir and the Secretary were still sitting in the same positions they were left in.

"Sorry, sir. It took a little longer," Lyman said to his boss. "Everything's set."

Harrison had a brief flash of recognition that he quickly quelled. Amir seemed not to notice.

"I'll be staying up here with you two tonight, and I brought—"

"Zak."

"Zak is going to stay here, too. And we added extra outside security. But most of the detail are getting caught up on some rest."

"Fine," the Secretary said.

Amir didn't say a word, which surprised Zak. His

eyes studied him, appearing to look for evidence he was carrying. Without a body search, Zak didn't think he'd find anything.

Lyman picked up a tray of dishes on the table between them, handing it to Zak. "You guys want anything else?"

"I'll take another juice," said Amir.

"Make it two," added Harrison.

In the kitchen, Lyman pulled Zak aside. "You take a little time in here, rinse the dishes, and tell Kyle we're in, no objections. Then I want you to make an obvious check of all the doors and windows. You find anything that looks funny, you scratch your head and we make eye contact, got it?"

"Yup."

Lyman left with two chilled bottles of pomegranate juice and two glasses.

Zak instructed Kyle and promised to get back to him on the hour.

"Got it. Everything cool so far out here." Kyle signed off, and Zak returned to the living room.

Lyman stood in the corner away from any of the windows or doors, nearly in the shadows. Zak nodded to him and began his house search. He listened to parts of the muffled conversation between the Secretary and Amir.

"So I guess we should start getting down to details,"

said Harrison.

Amir looked at Zak, who was checking the lock on French doors at the far end of the living room, which led out onto a patio. The blue light of the pool blanketed an eerie azure glow over the gardens below. He noticed a cat's wet footprints leading away from the balcony and around the corner.

"They have to stay," said Harrison. "These guys are government employees, used to this. I have no worries about them."

"Very well. I'd like to see the paperwork. And you have a package for me?"

"Yes, yes. But let's discuss the details first."

"Did you bring the contract *and* the package, Porter?"

"Yes. I have it in the next room. Relax, Youssef. Just what is causing all this worry on your part? Is it me, this situation, or something else? I need to know."

Amir sat back as if considering what to say. He was chewing on his lower lip and then flicking pieces of lint from his trousers. His expensive sweater, which probably cost more than most inhabitants of the island earned in a month, looked hot and out of place. His pumps were worn without socks. At last, he began. "I only have one shot at this, Porter. If I should fail, I'll need a quick evacuation from Morocco. That means I leave everything behind. There's the issue with my wife and children and their safety."

"Nothing you've said gives me pause. What are you up against? I sense some obstacle."

"No obstacle. I have to have assurances from you that my interests will be protected—in case things go wrong."

"Sure. That's part of the agreement."

"Which isn't official," said Amir with a hint of a smile.

"Of course not. This document will never see the light of day. The President and some of our senior staff, but that's all. It just outlines what our roles are here. Amir, am I missing something? Didn't we iron out all this earlier?"

"Yes. Okay, I'm ready to see the agreement and the package."

Zak had completed the doors and windows in the main living area. He headed toward the hallway that led to other rooms, including the Secretary's bedroom, and passed Harrison, who was carrying the tan rucksack he'd brought to town and a manila envelope.

"Everything clear in the front room, sir," Zak reported to the Secretary.

"Okay, good."

Zak peered into what appeared to be a workroom complete with fax machine, a large copy machine, and a bank of four computers and printers. He wasn't familiar with the phone lines and had expected them to not be landlines, but one phone had a light on, indicating use. He would have to find out who was online after he completed his check.

He finished the master and all the other support rooms, including three bathrooms and a huge walk-in closet banked in mirrored doors that was twice the size of his own apartment. A plush plum-colored leather chair was in the corner. The center of the room had a small three-foot by three foot carpeted pedestal. He noted a video camera mounted in the upper right corner with a flashing red light.

Cameras in a closet?

Remembering that the house was frequently used by a variety of guests and friends, he wouldn't rule out anything.

Coming back to the living room, he noted the rucksack was on Amir's side of the table, while the man was shuffling through some papers. Secretary Harrison was staring off toward the kitchen. Lyman caught his attention, and Zak nodded to both of them.

Lyman angled his head behind him, and Zak began the search of the other wing of the house, which housed additional rooms, including a video game room equipped with more machines than most arcades had.

He heard Amir speak behind him. "I will take this,

study it tonight and then give you my signed copy tomorrow."

"But," Harrison sounded concerned.

"No worries, Porter. I'm not going anywhere. I'll be here all night!"

Zak watched for Lyman to poke his head down the hall, but in the absence of that, he decided to notify Kyle of his search.

"Cleared the Secretary's wing, living, and dining rooms," he whispered.

"Roger that, Jell-O"

The timing was odd, but he was grateful for his LPO putting some levity into the situation.

"Stay loose but eagle eyes. Dead out here."

"Yessir."

The last door he knew led to the room where Amir would be staying. From the diagram he'd studied, it was also a suite, but on a less grand scale than the Secretary's. He turned the doorknob and was faced with a pitch-black room, except for the glow from the pool below. He bent down to the left to feel for a light switch, and he heard a pop. Then several more. Something whizzed over his head, traveling down the hallway and resulting in a shattering of glass in the living room behind him. These little projectiles propelled him backward, like someone was throwing marbles at him, hitting his vest.

What the fuck?

He suddenly lost his balance, falling back into the hallway. The black room on the other side of the gaping doorway was ominously silent, but behind him, he heard footsteps and the drawing of weapons. Someone was double-checking the rooms he'd already checked, dammit. He started to point to the black room to tell them they were searching the wrong area and couldn't feel his hand or his arm.

He heard the crackle in his ear. "Zak, you okay?"

"Nah. I'm hit, I think." Zak felt warm liquid transcending down his cheek and the unmistakable smell of blood.

Before he could finish his sentence, Kyle was in the hallway. "Hold on there, buddy. Lyman will be with you in a minute after he gets the Secretary secure. Coop's on his way, too." He hopped over Zak, sheltered, and then entered the room. A series of quick repeats, a loud flash, and then the sounds of broken glass scattering began as Zak felt the strong grip on his collar pulling him down the hallway toward the living room.

Fuck, if I'm gonna need medical attention, I want Coop or T.J. Give me one of my own guys. He felt lightheaded. It was getting difficult to hold his head up to see what had happened in the room. Blood was obscuring one eye. He used his right shoulder to try to wipe some of it away and wasn't successful. The trail from his body being dragged down the white carpet was blood red. He was starting to worry about how to get all that blood out when he heard a greeting that was familiar.

"Hello, Jell-O."

He was relieved to see Coop looking over him. His expression was flat as he examined his face.

"I can't move my arm. Can't feel my fingers, Co-op." Zak's voice broke like a kid in summer camp. Coop had turned him slightly, and his hand went to his backside and down the backs of his thighs.

"Fuck, Coop. Helluva time to tell me you're in love with me. We barely know each other."

He thought Coop would laugh and tell him something equally disrespectful, but Coop was all business. "Hold on. We got you. Nothing life-threatening, okay? So you just concentrate on that and let me do my job."

Distant sounds of automatic weaponry pierced the air.

I should be out there. I shouldn't be lying down here taking a nap. But he did feel tired.

"What happened, Coop?"

"I was hoping you could tell me."

"They were waiting for me in the room when I opened the door."

"Why do you say 'they'?"

"I don't know. Felt like someone was—"

"Coop, we gotta move him," Kyle ordered. "We got the shooter, but we think he has friends on the outside."

"Roger that, Kyle."

They both lifted Zak at the shoulders and ankles until he was set down on a large flowered couch. Coop kneeled at his side.

"Zak, this is important. Did you see anyone?"

"Fuck no. It was black. I turned to find the light switch. I fuckin didn't think to use my flashlight, and then I got hit."

Coop spoke over him to his LPO. "Probably saved his life."

"Okay, buddy, we've called for a rescue team, and as soon as we can, we're getting you off this fuckin' rock." Zak knew Kyle just enough to know when he meant business he talked faster, and he was talking very fast now, but not loud.

"So there was a shooter? Just one?"

"Hell yeah, Zak. I think you scared off the other one, if there was one," chuckled Kyle.

"If there had been two, you'd be dead. So would the Secretary and everyone else," added Coop.

"Where?"

"Lyman has them in the safe room. They're okay. But we're pulling extraction and getting him the hell out, too."

Zak turned his face and felt the ooze of more blood covering his chin, down his neck, and into his shirt. "God, the whole side of my face is starting to heat up, Coop. I must have gotten scraped with something. I think my right eye is swollen shut."

"I'm trying to stop the bleeding to check it out, Zak. Good news is I don't think they hit any internal organs."

"Where did I—" Zak felt himself get weak. Blackness moved across his remaining eye. He heard the hiss and crackling of something inside his head, and soon, all sound and light was gone.

CHAPTER 11

A MY WAS RELIEVED her dad's condition hadn't left extensive damage, and his rehab consisted mostly of rest, a non-vigorous routine with a personal trainer, and some dietary choices for now.

"I think you should have Marlene move in, Dad."

"Oh, Amy." His skin color had normalized. The nurses were talking about getting him up out of bed and trying some limited walking. It would be going on the second day after his heart attack without any signs of it returning.

"I think it would be wonderful if she stayed and could help take care of you."

"I'm not a goddamned invalid," Allister Dobson pouted.

It was another sign he was mending. He had a great sense of humor, and that had come back first. But the stubbornness was returning, too, which meant he was frustrated being constrained by anything.

"Dad, come on. You won't be able to do the things you used to do for a while. You'll have a nurse for part of the day, but what about the rest of the time? You could injure yourself. God forbid, you have another heart attack and you're all alone and can't get help."

"I don't want to be coddled along, *nursed* by my girlfriend. She's not my nurse. She doesn't have to take care of me."

"But she wants to, Dad. I've spoken with her."

"You have no right to offer my place to her." She could see her father was becoming agitated, and that worried Amy.

"I didn't offer it. She's come over a couple of times to check on me. We've had lunch together once there in the kitchen. Dad, she really wants to help. Let her do that, won't you?"

Chief Dobson crossed his arms and didn't look Amy in the eye.

She leaned over, kissed him, and squeezed his left hand. "Just think about it. She wants to help because she cares about you. Really cares about you."

"Amy, I don't want to be anybody's burden."

"Don't be ridiculous. You are far from a burden." She could see his stubbornness was stronger than hers because she was worried about him getting too agitated, and he wasn't. She decided to pull out her last card. "Dad, if you don't, I won't be able to go back down to

San Diego. I'll be required here. I can't just leave you all alone. I won't do that. *You* wouldn't do that for me."

"I'll consider it," he mumbled. "How long are you staying here?"

"That all depends on you, Dad. You going to follow doctor's orders or be stubborn?"

Amy's cell phone rang.

"I'm looking for Amy Chambers."

"This is she."

"This is Chief Petty Officer Collins. We haven't met yet, but I work with the guys on Kyle's Team."

"Is something wrong?"

Amy's father winced, holding his breath. The two of them locked eyes.

"I'm afraid Zak's been injured a few hours ago off the North African coast. He's been treated at a military facility in Morocco, but he's being airlifted to Germany."

"Oh my God!" Amy started to shake, taking a seat next to her dad's hospital bed. Her father buzzed his nurse's station alarm.

"He's alive, and he's going to recover. These weren't life-threatening injuries, but until we know more, I'm afraid I don't have much in the way of detail. I'm just letting you know."

One of the floor nurses came into the room. Her father whispered to her while Amy was occupied.

"Should I arrange to meet him in Germany?"

"Let's wait. Normally, we let them call you themselves. It's just that he's had a surgery and will be having more." He hesitated. "Kyle and the guys are kinda busy right now, and when he's available, I'll have him call you, too. Just wanted you to know and to know we'll update you just as soon as we have more to tell you. And we'll continue to do that, too, until Zak can call himself."

Amy couldn't think of anything to say and knew she'd have a ton of questions. She looked down at the phone. "Is this the number I can call you back on?"

"Yes, ma'am. And trust me, as soon as either Zak or Kyle or one of the guys can, I'll make sure they call you first thing, okay?"

"Okay."

"You might get in touch with Christy Lansdowne this afternoon. She can help you a lot. She's been through this a bunch of times."

"I'm up north in Santa Rosa. My father's had a heart attack."

"Oh gosh, I'm so sorry. Well, you'll want to be up there with your family, then. That's probably the best thing right now, anyway. But be sure to reach out to your LPO's wife."

"Mr.—Chief Petty Officer Collins, was it?"

"Yes, ma'am."

"What is the extent of his injuries?"

"I don't know the severity of it, but I believe he was shot in the thigh, his shoulder, and—his face received some injury. I'm not sure exactly sure what that means."

"But he's expected to recover. He's not critical."

"Oh no, Amy. Don't worry about that. He's coming home. I just don't know all the details yet. Once we do, we can be of more service, okay?"

"Thank you."

"Do you want me to have anyone else call you?"

"No." She thought about her father, who was waiting anxiously to find out the news. "Maybe there is someone you can have call. Armando's wife, Gina? Could you have her give me a call?"

"Well, I can't guarantee that since she's a spouse, and Armando is still on the mission, but let me see what I can do. I'm going to wait to hear from Kyle before I tackle that. And I'd tell Christy, also."

Amy began to babble. She apologized and hung up, clinging to the words, 'It's not life-threatening.'

CHAPTER 12

ZAK HEARD SHARP electronic hissing sounds at first and then someone calling his name and trying to move him. He didn't want to move. His body hurt in several places, like he'd fallen off a building. But his head hurt most of all.

More muffled sounds came from the room that was cold and bright as hell. A strong aftertaste lingered in his mouth, and his lips were parched. Someone was doing something to his arm. His name was called again. Finally, someone with horribly bad breath rudely pushed their face into his and tried to open his eyes. Or rather, one eye. A heavy bandage covered the other one. The puffy cheeked man had huge pores and red skin. Zak wanted to tell him to get off him and let him breathe.

"Zak, you're here in the hospital, and we've just completed a fairly extensive surgery, setting bones and working on your face. I need you to wake up. Can you do that, buddy?"

I'm not your fucking buddy. Get your ugly face outta my space. Did he say hospital?

His eyelid was swollen. When the guy pulled it back again, it hurt.

"Ouch!" Zak shouted, surprised at the strength of his own voice. He had a mind to reach out and grab the guy by his collar. He tried to lick his lips, but his tongue was stiff like shoe leather. He felt swelling on the right side of his face, extending from just under his eye all the way to his mouth, which was cracked and pulsing in pain.

"Yeah, I know it hurts. You'll be tender there, but I need you awake."

Zak's vision was blurry. He felt like his mouth had been stuffed with cotton that sucked all the spit out of him. His tongue was stuck to his top palate. He dislodged it and swallowed. That hurt, too.

"Son of a bitch," he said, sounding like the cotton was still there. "Wha? Wha happened? Where the fuck am I?"

"Well, you were flown here early this morning. You remember being on the island, yes?"

"Fuckin A."

"Okay, and you remember being shot? In the house?"

Oh yeah. He'd thought they were marbles. He was

thanking his lucky stars for the vest when he discovered he was bleeding. Coop was there...

"You were flown here to Germany. You're at Landstuhl," the voice said. "I'm Dr. Mavis. You're going to be our guest for awhile."

There was only thing Zak wanted to know. He couldn't feel his legs or his right arm. "Did you cut anything off?"

"No, Special Operator Chambers, just your clothes. But that doesn't mean you weren't severely injured, son."

Zak was again having a hard time focusing. "So what's wrong with me? You guys drop me out of a helicopter in the desert somewhere? That's how I feel."

Dr. Mavis sat down on the edge of the bed. His voice was gentler as they heard someone in the hallway screaming and swearing at the top of his lungs.

"Zak," the doctor said as he pressed his hand against his left shoulder. "You were shot in the leg, which shattered the bone there, so you've had some surgery to repair that. You won't feel that leg for a while. Your arm wasn't hurt as bad, but you did require a pin in one of the lower bones."

Zak knew there was something else the man didn't want to tell him.

"And?"

"Well, it's the injury to your face that I'm most

concerned about. The round must have ricocheted because we think it was a fragment that caught you right at the arch of your right eye; we call it the zygomatic arch. That bone was shattered. It tore a big hole there that'll need some skin grafting later on. We'll have to do some reconstructive surgery to your face." He touched him again on the shoulder before he stood beside the bed and folded his hands in front of him. "We aren't sure if we can save your right eye."

There it was. Zak was glad he was encumbered and couldn't get up, because he wanted to take something and throw it through the wall.

"My eye is still there?"

"Yes. But it's unhappy right now. Lots of pressure build-up already, which is not a good sign, son."

"You fuckin' mean it will explode or something?"

"Of course not. But you shouldn't be getting your blood pressure worked up, either. I know in your SEAL training they teach you how to control your emotions. We just need to do the same here. Give your body all the time it needs to heal. Your body is a wonderfully complicated and amazing machine. It can heal itself faster than I could. We just have to give it everything it needs right now. That means sleep, light movement, nothing strenuous. Patience."

"Did everyone get out okay?"

"I don't know anything of your mission or its outcome. All I know is that you weren't the only one who came in here from your team."

"Who else is here?"

"I don't have that. I was told to tell you that your LPO would be calling you tomorrow. For today, you just need to rest, Zak. And wait."

Of all the things he was tasked to do, waiting was the hardest.

"So when do I get to take a look at it?"

"Give it a day. Maybe two. I don't want to disturb anything in case we get a low-grade infection. It could affect your eye."

The doctor left.

Zak's room was set for four beds, but he was the only one in there. Maybe, if the other team guy wasn't too injured, they could share this room. He longed for someone to talk to, and he vowed he'd get the soldier's name and would work on that almost immediately.

He had two main concerns. First, he wondered what happened to the rest of his team, who were in the middle of a firefight when he was dragged backwards, leaving that bloody trail. And second, when should he contact Amy? Did the Navy do that? What would she think if she heard it on the news or from someone else before he talked to her?

He thought he should call, just to tell her he was alive. If she knew about the incident, she'd worry about him until she could talk to him in person. He buzzed the call button, and one of the male nurses came in with a clipboard.

"S.O. Chambers? Are you in pain?"

"No. I want to talk to my wife."

"Of course you do, but I can't authorize that, yet, sir."

"Can you check to make sure my cell is in my bag, then? Maybe charge it up for me?"

"If you promise me you'll not do anything heroic." He began checking a metal locker at the opposite wall. After rummaging through items in his black duty bag, the nurse stopped, closed the door, and shrugged. "Sorry, S.O. Chambers, but I don't see one in here."

"Fuck." He recalled the phone out and charging next to his bed when he showed up for his shift that night. He wished he could talk to Kyle or Cooper about it.

"I'll ask the doctor. I'm not sure you're supposed to be doing anything but resting. You're not to sit up or move around. You get to pee in that jar with the tubes and all."

Zak saw the plastic tubing filled with light yellow fluid extending out from under the covers at his waist.

"I told you. You don't even get up to go to the bathroom, so you gotta be patient."

"But she'll be worried about me."

"As most wives are. But the Navy will take care of all that. In due time, Chambers. In due time."

"He said someone else was here from my squad. Who?"

"He's right next door to you for now. Alex Kowicki's his name."

"Oh good." The room began to get blurry, and Zak became nauseous. He sighed and put his left hand on his stomach.

"You okay?"

"Feeling sick to my stomach. A little dizzy."

"Those are things you're supposed to avoid. You need to forget everything and just heal, just relax."

Ignoring him, Zak asked, "How's Kowicki?"

"Better than you," the nurse said and then broke a smile.

Zak began to move as if he was going to get out of bed.

"Whoa, whoa there, cowboy. You're to stay perfectly still, because it increases the chances your eye will heal, understand me? Don't go moving that head or putting any pressure doing anything. That eye is in bad shape. You're supposed to just lie back and try to get caught up on your rest. Your time for moving around, rehab, will come. But it's way too soon now."

Zak felt like someone had pounded his chest and face while he was asleep. The surgery had him swollen, and his face and cheek felt hot.

"I'll see when you can have some broth. You were in surgery for several hours yesterday. The anesthesia is just wearing off. I know it's a crappy feeling. You want something to make you sleep?"

"No. I want to be awake in case someone has news. I need to know what happened to the rest of the team. And I need to call my wife, dammit."

The warmth in his face was pulsing now. A headache was beginning to come on strong. He knew if he stayed awake he'd be focusing on the pain.

"Changed my mind. Knock me out."

Maybe when he woke up this whole fuckin' dream will have turned out to just be a nightmare. Maybe this wasn't really happening, he thought as the drug relaxed him to the point he couldn't keep his eyes open any longer.

CHAPTER 13

A MY RETURNED TO her father's house. She'd driven her dad's car. Pouring herself a glass of wine, she sat at the kitchen table remembering all those past family discussions about going to college and her relationship with Zak in high school. Her parents had been so worried about her getting pregnant.

"There's a whole beautiful world out there, Amy. More than just sex and parties. Don't throw your life away," her mother had said.

Then she thought about Zak's parents. She'd gotten so worked up about the news she hadn't even considered them. She picked up the phone and took a sip of her wine, waiting for the phone to connect.

"Gloria, this is Amy. I'm afraid I have some bad news." Amy didn't see any point in dancing around the issue.

Mrs. Chambers took in a deep breath. "Is he—?"

"Injured. Not dead."

"Oh, thank God!" Amy heard her scramble for a chair. She also heard Jack Chambers whisper a question in her ear.

"He's alive, but injured, Jack. Let me get the details."

"He's in Germany. Apparently, he was shot several times. Has a leg and arm injury—and a face wound of some kind." Amy felt the tears begin to well up. Her lower lip was trembling. She was trying to be strong, show confidence to the parents of the man she loved. It's what he'd want her to do.

"But for sure he's going to be okay, right?" Mrs. Chambers drilled.

"Yes." Amy wasn't even convinced of this. "I will feel a lot better when I can talk to him. They said someone would be in touch with me soon. I'll make sure I let you know just as soon as I do, okay?" Now she wanted to be off the phone. Any questions they'd have were the same ones she'd have, and she wasn't sure how long before she'd break down, and that wasn't acceptable.

"So the face wound, is it serious?"

"The Chief didn't explain. I'm supposed to get an update soon."

"Thank you, Amy. You have some friends you can stay with until you hear an update?" Gloria's comment caught Amy by surprise. She was touched by the fact that Zak's mother was more concerned for her own well being than her own.

"I have Marlene here." And then she realized she hadn't told them about her father. "I'm sorry! I am up here in Santa Rosa. My father had a heart attack yesterday."

"Oh, Amy! I'm so sorry. Oh, you poor dear. What can I do?"

"He's resting comfortably. They're still running tests and such. His girlfriend is coming over. I just came from there. That's where they called me."

"Listen, honey, please feel free to come over here and let our home be yours."

"Thank you very much. I appreciate it. But I'm housesitting at my dad's. I want to know he's going to be safe before I go back. I need to get to San Diego as soon as possible."

"Yes, you need to be with those, those..." Gloria Chambers began to cry. "Oh, this is all so sad."

Amy knew she was missing her boy and wanted to be there to take care of him, just as Amy did. Any mother would want to be rushing to his side. And yet, the woman was respectful of her place. That was now Amy's job. But veiled in her comments about "those people" was that Zak belonged to the SEAL community. Yes, he was her son, but he belonged to them.

Amy had the same sadness. Nothing she could do.

Nowhere to go. She had to be patient and wait. It was all out of her hands. What she had to do was stay strong. That gave her the courage to say, "Gloria, how about if I come over tomorrow morning for coffee? We can talk. I'll give you any updates. Perhaps we could call Zak, if they'll let us. Would you like that?"

Amy couldn't understand what Gloria Chambers was saying as the woman sobbed into the phone. Jack Chambers' voice came on the line.

"My wife would like that very much, and so would I."

Amy called Christy Lansdowne next. She could hear the kids in the background, T.V blaring, sounding like she had more than just their three.

"Wait a minute, Amy." Christy shouted some brief commands, and the house was silent. "I mean it, the T.V. will be off for the rest of the week if you guys raise your voices again." She came back to the phone. Amy heard the unmistakable sound of ice cubes in a glass. "How's your dad?"

"Much better, thanks. It's a mix-up of his medication. I hope to be coming back to San Diego soon."

"That's good news."

"Listen, I have some bad news."

"Oh no. What is it, girlfriend?"

"Has Chief Collins called you?"

"No, ma'am. Why, is there a problem?"

"He called me to say there had been an incident, and Zak was injured and airlifted to Germany. He's not critical, Christy. He didn't know anything else, but suggested I call you."

"Did he say anyone else was hurt?"

"Yes, someone else went over with Zak. But the guys were still in the field so he said Kyle would call when he could. Just was wondering if he'd called you."

Christy took another sip of her drink. "No. Oh, this is the bad part, Amy. This is the worst of it. We wait. We don't know what to do, so we pretend to go about our day as usual, for the sake of the kids and their routine. We don't scare them with our own worries or fears. And sometimes—"

Amy could tell she had begun to cry. At last Christy sniffled, blew her nose, and composed herself.

"Not a very good example, am I?"

"You're a perfect example."

"What I was going to say was that sometimes when we just go about our own routines, it helps. Like pretending it's okay makes it so. Kind of Zen, I know, and unlike me, but I can't help it. It works."

"Thanks, Christy."

"You poor angel. Zak's first deployment, too. On top of your dad's heart attack. Well, thank God your guy's okay."

"Yes, thank God for that. I know they did everything they could to keep him safe. But that's all I have."

"Well, we are all the team that stays behind. Don't forget that. Something happens, we close ranks."

"I'm learning."

"You poor baby. I'll bet you didn't want to upset your dad, either."

"No. Chief Collins called when I was visiting my father in the hospital. I didn't follow the rules and turn it off. But you know, with Zak and all—"

"Just what I would have done. Okay, here's what we'll do. I'm babysitting tonight. Got six here right now. Banking the babysitting points so Kyle and I can take a nice couple of days together somewhere when he gets back. I'll start making calls to see if I can find out anything. If Collins knows anything, I'll dig it out of him with a rusty spoon!"

Amy chuckled. "Thanks, Christy."

"No, it's what I do. It's my job. So if I get any news at all, I'll call you. Keep your phone by your side day or night. If I can get through to someone who will let Zak call you, I'll do that. They're on a different time zone there, so that's why you have to be prepared, okay?"

"Yes, ma'am."

"You're so sweet. I want to hug you and wipe away all your tears until we learn the good news. You just don't worry about a thing. Focus on your dad, and put this all out of your mind. Don't you worry. Everything's going to be all right."

"I can't thank you enough. You live up to your reputation, Christy."

"What's that?"

"Mama bear. Gina told me to get used to it."

"Gina's one tough lady. The strongest of our bunch."

"If you call her, would you tell her I'd like some advice?"

"Sure. Can I ask what?"

"My dad. I think they're going to ask him to retire. Medically retire. Maybe Gina can give me some perspective on what that does to a career cop, other than the few of my dad's friends who have drunk themselves under the table. Something he could look forward to. I'm sure she's seen it."

"I'll do it. I'll see if she got any calls." Christy paused. "You don't know who the other person was who was injured?"

"No, but from the sound of it, I'm fairly sure it wasn't Kyle. But that's just a guess, Christy."

"Gotcha. Okay. Time to get these guys into their pajamas and get ready to be picked up. I've got calls to make. You take care."

"Thanks so much. I feel better already."

"Good. Mission accomplished, for now."

Amy wondered if she'd ever be able to flip that imaginary switch. Because of what had happened on Zak's first deployment, there would always be worry on her end. She wondered if Kyle had ever been injured and how Christy handled it. Or how she handled—

Maybe that was too much to think about. Christy had ordered her to put everything else out of her mind and focus on her dad. Well, she'd add Zak's mother and father to that responsibility; they were now her family, too.

CHAPTER 14

THE TEAM OF doctors in white coats descended on Zak as he was waking up from a mid-morning nap. He'd learned to depend on his left eye more and more. The vision he had was improving. At the sight of the team, Zak became excited, sure that there would be some good news. That meant he could be discharged from the hospital sooner than later. That also meant he could finally call Amy. Get some news about his other teammates. He'd learned Alex had been transferred to another ward this morning. He regretted not being able to talk with him before he left.

The bandage was removed, but he still couldn't see and thought perhaps they'd not removed everything. He waited for them to do so.

The doctors came closer. Dr. Mavis began, "See, this is healing up nicely. We anticipate some grafting here and here. The hairline can be transplanted.

Hairline?

"Zak, can you see anything out of your right eye right now?"

"No. Take the fuckin' eye patch off and then maybe I'll see." He felt his temperature rise. He wanted to sit up, but someone pressed his shoulder back into the mattress. "Hairline? You said replace my hairline?"

"Can you see any light or flashes of light, Zak?" another doctor asked.

"No. But—"

"How about headaches? Do you have a headache now or did you wake up with one?"

"Of course I fuckin' woke up with one. You guys were pounding on my head it feels like for hours."

"Calm down, Zak. We're only here to help."

"Well, I will, as soon as you tell me about this hairline thing." He searched from one face to another and another like a cyclops. All of them were somber. He wasn't getting through to any of them. "What the fuck's the matter with you? I want to know what I look like. Don't you think I have a right to know?"

Dr. Mavis stepped closer to him. "You want to see it. All of it? We have a lot to explain."

"Yes, I want to see it. You're telling me I have to go buy a wig or get a hair transplant. I want to see how bad it is."

"Okay, Zak." Dr. Mavis extended his arm, and one of the nurses in the room handed him a mirror.

"Prepare yourself, Zak."

He knew before he put the mirror in front of his face he wasn't going to like what he saw. The person peering back at him was a Cyclops. His image appeared as scared as Zak felt. His pee flowed and he nearly lost what might be in his bowels. His blood pressure rose as he tried to make sense of the maze that was his face, twisted and red and covered in black stitches.

The black and blueing had begun, and he knew it would get much worse before it got better. Yellow and orange solutions had been spread all over his face and stitches, splashed on his forehead and chin. Mounds of red flesh were tied together like a roast. The wound began almost three inches into his hairline where there was no hair, just angry bruised skin. A drain he hadn't felt before extended from a spot just above where his eyebrow should have been. The stitching extended from the top of his crown, around his eye socket, and ended up in a crescent below what would have been his cheekbone. Except that was concave, oozing in spite of the stitches. His eyelid was nearly black, engorged so that it resembled a small dark purple plum. The right side of his lips were drawn up in a grimace, showing even the upper gum line, as the stitches attempted to connect the repair to his cheek with the rest of his lower facial skin.

It was worse than just the hairline issue. He was a

monster. And no matter how well it healed, he could see he would forever be a monster. He'd look like one of those guys on the Wounded fundraiser sites. Except they probably wouldn't use his face, because it would scare the kids. It would scare anyone. It would for sure scare Amy.

It scared the hell out of him.

The mirror fell from his hands. Hot tears flowed from the left eye only. He had no sensation in his right. The blackness was without reprieve. The harsh reality of his current medical condition crept up on him, making a sneaky little cackling sound. Telling him he was an idiot to expect the fame and honor and glory of being a SEAL. He'd been altered, damaged, and would never be the same.

He heard someone sobbing and realized it was he. His breath hitched as the air sputtered in and out from his mouth, from lips that would not close. One of the doctors patted him on the shoulder.

"Zak, we know it's a lot to take in. We are going to do everything within our power to improve the appearance. We have lots of things we can do, but you'll be in for a whole stream of surgeries. We can't do much more until we find out about that eye. There's a good chance you're going to lose it, Zak."

"Go away. Leave me alone," Zak sobbed. What he wanted to say was, "Go away and let me die," but he was too proud to do so.

He felt something cool go into his arm. He would have felt grateful if he knew the drug would take away his monster face. But nothing could do that. Now a freak, a victim of some crazy's gun, battered, soul shaken, he just couldn't quit.

He might not look like one, but he was still a SEAL.

CHAPTER 15

A MY GOT THE call she'd been waiting for at three am.
"Amy, this is Kyle."

She bolted out of bed. "Kyle! Is he okay? How badly is he hurt? When can I talk to him? Should I get a ticket and come to Germany?"

"Hold on, Amy. I understand you are in Santa Rosa. Sorry to hear about your father."

"He's going to be okay, Kyle. But why haven't I heard from Zak?"

"He's hurt pretty bad, Amy. I haven't seen him yet, but I've been talking to his medical team. We're going to try to see him in a week if we can wrap up things here."

"Hurt bad? I understand he was shot in the leg? Oh my God, he isn't going to lose his leg, is he?"

"No, Amy. That's all going to be okay. His leg and arm are fine. We're used to this kind of trauma over here, unfortunately."

"So what? You said he was hurt bad. You mean his face injury is bad?"

"Yes, unfortunately."

She was sweating, streams running down from her armpits. Her heart pounded, sending a deafening roar to her ears. Her fingers trembled as she clutched the phone. She switched it to speakerphone so the booming in her ears didn't block the signal. Her voice was unrecognizable, frog-like and shaky. "Tell me, Kyle."

"He may lose his eye. He's had a lot of reconstructive surgery to his face and will have to have lots in the months, perhaps years, to come. It's a long difficult road, Amy. You're going to have to be very, very strong for him."

Her world collapsed. Every single one of her fears, the things she'd pushed outside her head, came rushing in.

Blind. He'll be blind in one eye. But he'll be alive!

She clung to the good news. "Kyle, I'm in it for the long haul. We'll get through it. I know we will."

"I'm glad you feel that way, Amy. We're going to see about getting you over here to Germany, and I'm going to talk to Zak about it when I see him. In the meantime, he's being kept very quiet, so he gives his eye the best chance of recovery. They aren't letting him get up or move much. They want him to rest. There's a huge risk of infection, too, so they're monitoring the surgery. Lots of stitches, Amy. I'm told over a hundred, counting the ones on his leg and forearm."

"A hundred?"

"Yes. He got pretty badly beat up. He's lucky to be alive. The projectile was a high velocity type. If it had hit him square anywhere, it would have left a hole the size of my fist. But we think it ricocheted, and that slowed it down. Even then, it did a lot of soft tissue damage, and that's why the eye was affected."

"But he hasn't lost his eye."

"No. But we're not sure if it will survive. You'd best be prepared for a long convalescence and a lot of difficult days for Zak. He's not going to like what he gets. And he's going to need someone strong to help him get through it."

She'd signed on to this. She'd promised. Said she could handle it. It wasn't what she'd planned, but she knew in her heart she had the strength to deal with it.

"Now, tell me about your dad. What's the latest?"

"He was trying to be the last Latin lover. New girl-friend, you know. He was taking some herbal Viagra, and even though it says he shouldn't take it without notifying a doctor, my dad, well, he's stubborn. Plus, he's on blood pressure medication."

"I can totally understand, Amy. So he's ready to come home soon, then?"

"Yes. And though I'd love to stay, he has a girlfriend who wants to dote on him. I'm hoping Gina will help me invent some argument to allow her to do this. Then I can come back to San Diego."

"Good. Well, I hope that works out. You need to be back there. It will be awhile before Zak gets here, but there are things you're going to have to look into and resources we have as a community. We need to make sure all the ducks are in a row for his rehab. Our work is done here, and we're just finishing up a few things, doing some advisory things I can't talk about. So we'll probably be home sooner than we thought."

"How did it go?"

"You know I can't talk about that."

"Yes. Sorry." She sighed. Her heart had calmed down a little. Suddenly, the fierce talk with her dad didn't seem like such a big thing to her.

"You okay? Make sure you remember who and what you are. You're the wife of a Navy SEAL. He picked you because you are strong. You already proved that with the San Francisco terrorist attack. This is a different kind of strength. And there's the issue of Zak and how he feels."

"I know him. He loves his SEAL community and the brotherhood. It's the most important thing in his life."

"We don't live forever and things happen. He's alive. We just want him to have the best future he can have. And we want you a part of that, too. We don't leave anyone behind, even if they are no longer SEALs. They're still part of the family."

Amy tried not to let Kyle's words distress her. But she heard loud and clear; he was telling her Zak might be so injured that he wouldn't be able to serve. On top of losing an eye, that could be perhaps the biggest wound of all.

THREE HOURS LATER, she got another call. "Amy, this is Gina. Christy told me about Zak. I'm so sorry, honey. Is this too early to call? I understand you're in California?"

"Yes. Thanks so much."

"What can I do for you?"

"Sorry, Gina. I'm a little out of it this morning." Amy checked the clock beside the bed. Marlene was supposed to drop by for a few minutes to get some things for her father. Then she was going to meet with the Chambers before going to the hospital. The call with Kyle was a distant memory. Did it really happen? Her eyes were puffy now. Yes, it had happened, and she'd cried herself to sleep afterwards.

She had just enough time to shower and throw on some clothes. "I overslept. So I'm glad you called. Wow."

"Oh God, Amy. I can't imagine what you're going

through, and all by yourself, with your dad in the hospital. You're wise to get rest. You've been hit with a double whammy. So tell me how I can help."

Amy wondered how much of Zak's condition Gina knew.

"Well, with this heart attack, his doctor mentioned to me he was going to recommend my dad retire. As you know, being the Chief of Police here in Santa Rosa, you can imagine, he'd rather have all his teeth pulled from his skull without anesthesia."

"Yeah, a dedicated man. One of the good guys."

"Exactly. So I wondered if you could give me any tips on convincing him."

"Boy, that's a tough one, Amy. Let me ask you this. Does he have a life outside his police work?"

Amy was going to keep his secret, but she'd already let Kyle in on it, so she reluctantly answered Gina's question truthfully. "He has a girlfriend. That's how he got into all this mess with the herbal Viagra. It interfered with his blood pressure medications. He's trying to be a thirty-year-old man again."

Gina laughed. "How old is your dad?"

"Sixty-seven."

"He have a protégé? Someone he feels good about passing the baton to?"

"Not that I know of. No, I think he figured he'd die in that job." The word stuck in her throat, and tears threatened.

"We don't say that. That's not going to happen."

"Sorry." She knew Gina was right.

"Too bad his girlfriend couldn't sort of distract him, lure him with tales of sailing off to exotic places. You know, honey bee stuff."

"I'm sure she'd be good at it."

"I think that's your ticket. I can't think of any logical reason he'd want to retire, unless he expected to do something more fulfilling in the future. Does that help?"

"Yes, it does. Can they force him to retire like that? I mean, if the doctor writes something up, does he even have a say in the matter?"

"He might find ways to suppress that information, but no, he's past retirement age. A lot of guys go out on disability and then retire."

"I've heard of that. Don't think he'll do that. He'll hang on as long as he can."

"Then you get the girlfriend in on it. You like her?"

"She's great. Wonderful woman. A little younger."

"All the better."

"She and I get along well. We're only about fifteen years apart. And she has no family of her own."

"I think you have your solution."

"Thanks, Gina. You heard from Armando?"

"Yes, he called me just before I dialed you. They

had a rough go over there. The other SEAL injured is being released today and flying home."

"Who is it?"

"Alex, you know, one of the bachelors who used to live with Lucas?"

"I met him at the Cooper's party."

"Yes, and he was at the wedding, too."

"So when did he say they come home?"

"Not sure. Maybe two weeks, or less. I hope less. The baby could come at any time."

Amy admitted to herself she was a bit jealous.

She heard a car outside. "Gina, I have to run, but thanks so much."

"For what? I didn't do anything."

"Yes, you did. I'll be back down there as soon as I get my dad situated."

"You let me know. Amy, we'll all help you. We do this together. Just want you to know you are not alone. You're one of us now."

She could hardly sign off, there were so many tears.

After hanging up the phone, she collected herself, wiped her cheeks, and jumped into the shower. Amy needed the strength the warm water would give her, as well as a place to finish her crying. She knew Marlene would use her key to get in.

She was drying off when Marlene poked her head in. "Sorry." She covered her eyes.

"Oh, please. Don't be silly. I'll be right out."

Dressed and clean, Amy went in search of Marlene and found her in the kitchen making coffee.

Marlene's red hair and coral lipstick set off her peachy complexion. Amy could see why her father was so smitten with her. Her young vibrance would be good for him, she thought. Thinking about the bounce in her father's step, she realized she hadn't seen it for several years, ever since her mother started her slow decline and eventual death from cancer. She cheerily brought Amy a steaming cup of coffee loaded with cream, just like she liked it.

Amy finally put into words what she'd been grasping for. "Thanks, Marlene. It's been wonderful having you here. Makes all this with my dad easier for me."

"Ahh, sweetie," Marlene said, setting down her own coffee cup. With a palm to Amy's cheek, she said, "Anything I can do to help, name it. You know I think the world of your dad, and taking care of you, too, is just part of what I love doing. Never had my own family, something I now regret."

The two women hugged.

"How're you holding up, hmm?" Marlene brushed the hair from Amy's face, angling her head to the left and studying her carefully.

"Zak's LPO, that's—"

"I know what that is."

"Well, Kyle called me early this morning, and Zak might lose his eye. He's got a lot of facial reconstruction ahead of him. Surgeries and the like. His leg and arm will be okay, but his face, especially the eye—" Amy broke off and turned her back to Marlene.

Sadness slipped between the two of them as Amy began to miss her mother, and she felt hot tears on the brink of bursting. Marlene kept her distance, sensing her need to be private and careful. "You go ahead and cry, sweetie. You have a lot to deal with right now."

Come on, Amy! Where's that strength you told Kyle you had?

She ground her teeth and turned back to Marlene. "There's a lot for me to prepare for in San Diego. I'm not going to be able to stay here much longer. I have to be there when Zak comes home. They might even get me on a plane to go see him in Germany and travel back to the states with him."

"I understand. Don't worry about Allister. I've got him taken care of."

"You know how stubborn my dad can be."

"Oh, I know, yes!" Marlene's eyebrows rose as she sipped her coffee. "He covers up a tender heart."

"I had a frank discussion with his doctor yesterday, and he indicated he might write up a recommendation he retire. I brought up his convalescence to Dad, and he thinks he'll be back to work as soon as he gets out of the hospital. But the doctor says definitely not."

Amy took her coffee mug and collapsed into a chair at the dining table facing the kitchen. Marlene took a seat across from her, her unwavering eyes showing strength. "I agree. I think he should start to retire before the job kills him. The pills are one thing, but it was the kind of scare we all should pay attention to, especially him. I'm going to work on that, Amy."

"He also doesn't want anyone being his nurse. Thinks he can do it all himself."

"I've already heard this two or three times. This is nothing new, sweetheart. I'm ready for him."

Amy was relieved. Marlene had the backbone she'd hoped for. Recalling her conversation with Gina, a crooked smile formed on Amy's face.

"Whatever are you thinking, Amy?"

"My friend suggested you would be the ticket to get my father out of the station. I think she was right."

Marlene leaned back in her chair, a hint of a blush streaking across her cheeks. "We have a healthy sexual relationship. I hope you're okay with hearing that. He doesn't really need the pills. I guess it's my job to make him understand and then to believe that." She wiggled her eyebrows. "Not a bad problem to work on, right?"

But Amy wasn't thinking about her dad and Marlene in the bedroom. She was wondering what it would be like to have Zak home.

CHAPTER 16

THE NURSE BROUGHT Zak an unexpected visitor, Alex Kowicki.

"Hey there, stud, you looking for sympathy from the pretty nurses with all your bandages and shit?"

Zak held up his three finger salute.

"So that answers *that* question."

"What question, asshole?" Zak was surprised even the sight of Alex didn't cheer him up.

"Well, see, there's two kinds of patients. There are good patients who do everything the doctors tell him to do. They get better, make everyone around them feel better, and no one likes to see them go. And then there are nasty patients, and a lot of men are this way. When they go—"

"You seen what my face looks like?" Zak interrupted.

"Of course not. You're into show and tell now? What am I supposed to do, Zak? I came by here to pay my respects."

"I'm not dying."

"You sure?"

"Shut the fuck up."

"Why didn't I see this before? You were never this ornery. Or were you?"

"I never looked like a freak. Maybe I'm just matching my insides with my outsides."

"Your choice, man."

Zak wished he could sit up. "Look, Alex. Thanks for coming. I'm not very good company. They won't even let me sit up yet. I can't do anything but lie here."

"Read a good book. You want me to get some of those raunchy German flesh magazines?"

"Read. With one eye?"

Alex sat down, letting out a puff of air. "Zak, you don't know you're going to lose the eye. At least you haven't lost your legs or hands. At least you don't shit in a colostomy bag every day because your guts were all blown up. You're not in a wheelchair for Chrissakes."

Zak's ego couldn't stand any more of it. He ripped the tape off his facial bandage, flung it to the floor and sat up, despite the warnings not to. "I could get a job in Hollywood with this fuckin' face!"

Alex stood up, swallowing, trying to hide his shock. It was something Zak knew was impossible to do.

"So you tell me now I should be grateful I survived.

Go ahead. Give me that stupid 'oh, it could have been worse' shit."

"Dayam, Jell-O. I think you're right. You'd be perfect for a zombie movie. To hell with the SEALs. You do have a new career ahead of you."

Zak reached for his water pitcher and threw it at Alex, missing. The plastic container hit the wall next to the open doorway, water splashing all over the floor and out into the hallway.

"Now get the fuck out and leave me alone."

Nurses began to enter the room. They summoned housekeeping and began scolding Zak about his removal of the bandage. He lay back, closed his one eye, and listened for Alex's departure.

AT NOON, THEY allowed him to sit up to eat a soft meal of cottage cheese and applesauce. He got his choice of custard or ice cream for dessert and asked for both. *Nothing wrong with my appetite.*

Shortly after lunch, a brown package arrived with four Playboys and two Hustler magazines, without a note attached.

ZAK STOPPED ASKING for the chance to call Amy. He'd even stopped asking where his cell phone was located. Days passed, and although he did think about what Amy must have been told, he stopped wanting to talk to her. He told himself it was so he could gather his thoughts. How could he talk to her? Say *'I'm coming home soon but brace yourself, I'm a fuckin' Cyclops. A freak.'*

I'll call her after we know about the eye.

It was a waiting game. Each day the same, mostly taken up with rest. He was allowed more movement gradually and celebrated the day he could take a shower with the help of a male aide. He avoided mirrors, even though his face was bandaged.

He had lots of time to think about the choices he'd made. Maybe he should have expected the shooter in that room. Why didn't he pay more attention to the light he saw on the telephone? That told him someone else was in the house. It could have been the help, but it could have also been the shooter, giving directions.

Hell, they could have all been killed with that kind of lapse. He fisted his hand and banged his thigh, forgetting about the stitches and the healing bone underneath, and it hurt like a son of a gun.

If he'd only searched the balcony first, perhaps he'd have found footprints just like the cat's. Maybe noticed the lack of a light coming from under the door. If he had crouched, sheltered before he opened the door, they would have missed him all together.

No, it was his fate to be the one Kyle chose. Would someone else have done it differently? The lump in his throat was difficult to swallow, and he was ashamed to wish his injury on any other of his team. Perhaps someone else wouldn't have been so lucky. It could have been fatal.

Over the next few days, he could tell the healing was happening. The skin was less hot and puffy. His lips were able to touch in a straight line. The headaches had stopped, and he prayed that meant the pressure on his right eye was lessened. Tiny rays of hope began to creep into his daily daydreams. Instead of causing pain, reliving some of the nice moments of his life made him feel better. He recalled the wedding and the way Amy kept her wits about her with the terrorist attack in San Francisco. He thought about his team and the Brotherhood. Happier times when he and the guys would play some trick on each other or get into one of those not-so-politically-correct conversations, the smacktalk that both irritated and strengthened them. He worried about his parents.

Zak read the SEAL prayer every morning, clinging to the belief he could somehow stay on the Team. After all, Joel had done it.

But there were also days when these visions were not helping. In fact, they made him feel worse. He never knew which it would be, and that irritated him, too.

A few days later, over a week after the accident,

Kyle walked into the room. Zak was in sitting position, reviewing one of the magazines Alex had dropped off. His mood was black today but he worked to try not to show it.

"I hear you're a real asshole as a patient."

"Afraid so." Zak returned his focus back to the magazine.

"Why the hell are you being so difficult? You're not cooperating with the people here who only want you well. You think that's gonna make you heal any faster?"

"Nah. Just trying to deal with it. I think I'm settling down a bit. Been two days since I threw something."

"You talk to Amy yet?"

"Um—" He quickly glanced around for one of the staff. "My cell phone seems to be missing, and I've not asked for a couple of days now. They told me no at first. But now they're letting me sit up a bit."

"Which reminds me, we got your Sig Sauer and your M4. I'll bring them stateside when we leave. But I don't remember seeing a cell phone."

"That day I left it in to charge."

"Sorry, there was a lot going on. I'm guessing the Canary Civil Guard has it."

"Right." Zak was watching Kyle's every movement, watching for signs he had been asked to "have that talk" with him about his future on the Teams.

Kyle paced back and forth, stopped, and said, "I've

talked to her."

Zak's stomach lurched. The razor cut a male aide made this morning while shaving him hurt all of a sudden. "How much does she know?"

"Everything I knew at the time. I think the doctors are calling her. Christy and Gina have been in touch. I guess I should tell you her father had a heart attack."

"Really? Oh, I'm sorry." He knew she must be hurting, but he couldn't feel anything. His capacity to hear about more pain and suffering had been depleted. It concerned him. "That didn't come out right. Tell her for me I'm sorry that I haven't been able to call. And I'm sorry about her dad, too. Is he okay?"

"He is. I think she's ready to come back to San Diego, or might be there now. Christy says she's coping with everything like a champ. But you knew that, didn't you?"

He did, but wasn't going to admit it. He tossed the magazine onto a chair to his left. "So the old man's going to recover?"

"Yes. He has to slow down. They're trying to convince him he should retire. I hear that's a hot topic with him."

"Know how he feels." He regretted saying it the instant it left his mouth. He glanced up at Kyle immediately. Kyle was looking away.

It was dangerous to bring it up, but the big elephant in the room was the fact that perhaps Zak would be medically discharged from the Teams. He wondered if that meant he had to go serve out the rest of his time in the regular Navy. He didn't want that news.

"We wait and see what happens with your eye. I have to tell you, Zak, a one-eyed sharpshooter is very rare."

"So I become a medic. Or I work the radio, do explosives."

"Well, we'll talk. You're an asset to the Teams, no doubt about that. Tough break to get it on your first round. Most of this decision is up to the Navy, sorry to say, but we'll think positive. That always helps in times like these."

"Roger that." Zak knew Kyle had reservations about him being able to continue. He was sorry he steered the conversation in that direction. "So never did hear how the mission went. Did everyone get out alive?"

"There are a couple of Moroccan's who were returned to the source. Amir is lying low. The Secretary is convinced he wasn't as innocent as he came across, or at least made some side deals with someone who couldn't be trusted. The Canary Island Civil guards were hardasses and wanted a full report before they'd let any of us leave the island. Get this—they even detained the Secretary of the United States!"

"No shit?"

"They didn't call it that, of course. State got to deal with them since it was their crazy idea."

"Give peace a chance?"

"My ass. Anyway, you'll get a commendation you won't read about anywhere since we were never there. But the Secretary wanted me to extend his gratitude on behalf of both he and Amir."

"Well, that's something, then."

"Zak, you do know you took the bullet that was meant for Amir, right?"

"I kinda thought so."

"Without your sacrifice, this could have been a real international incident."

"It's an incident all right. Just praying, Kyle, that my eye comes back."

Kyle was fidgeting with the weave on the blanket covering Zak. "There is one other thing I need to discuss with you."

Zak braced himself.

"In cases like this, where you'll need another surgery, perhaps before they release you, they do fly in the spouses. I think Amy wants to come. Should I arrange that, Zak?"

"Let's hold off a while on that."

"You should call her."

"I know it. When I'm ready. They haven't given me

the green light for that, and don't you tell her if they do. I want to be ready."

"You need to share it with her. She's the one who is going to be there right beside you. She's strong. Amy's a strong woman. You're lucky, Zak."

Zak flipped up the bandage that had loosened at the bottom edge from him scratching his stitches with his left forefinger. "You still think I'm lucky?" he said as he watched Kyle take a step back. "Would you show this to Christy?"

Kyle cleared his throat and then forced down a swallow, but didn't take his eyes off Zak's wounds. "Well, this is the worst it's gonna be, right?" He cleared his throat for the second time. "Gets better from here. The docs say you're in for some plastic surgery, once the bones heal. Maybe they can do a couple of tucks here and there. Who knows? Maybe you'll come back as Rock Hudson or something. They can work miracles."

The attempt at Kyle's dark humor fell flat and angered him a little. Zak dropped the flap and turned away from his LPO. "I'm not ready," he said to the wall.

Who the fuck wants to look like Rock Hudson?

CHAPTER 17

AMY RETURNED TO San Diego a week after Zak's injury, and upon seeing the blue water and the lovely community of Coronado, she felt relieved to be back. Issues with her father were working out. Marlene was going to move in, as Amy had suggested, and for now, her dad was going to come back on limited duty, only two days out of the week. The Department hired a temporary Assistant Chief to help with the duties when he wasn't available.

One war fought and temporarily won; one to go.

She asked lots of questions when Chief Collins stopped by. Zak would be returning in a week. He offered her a seat on a transport plane to Germany, so she could return with Zak.

"When can I talk to him?" The absence of communication between them was bothering her. "Is he avoiding me?"

"No. I don't think so. He was pretty banged up,

Amy. Not sure he's able to right now. He's been in and out of surgery lately, I understand."

"I'm not going unless I can talk to him."

Collins broached the subject of Zak retiring on disability from the military, since his injuries were combat-related. "And we have excellent VA benefits here in San Diego. He has his choice of several specialty centers."

"What about his eye?"

"Not sure yet. I haven't heard." Collins stood tall. He pointed to the brochures he'd left in front of her at the kitchenette table. "There's a whole list of what procedures are covered and not covered. He will require plastic surgery to his face."

"Is he automatically off the Teams?"

"Not officially, no. But, Amy, I think you'd better brace yourself for that eventuality, like I said earlier."

The experience she'd just had with her father came to mind. "It will be hard on him to quit, Chief Collins. Will he be forced to leave the SEALs?"

"That's not up to me. If he can get well enough, and if some of his eyesight comes back at least, I think we can save his spot. Without that, I'm afraid he'll be required to retire."

Amy had learned Zak wasn't going to need assistance walking. He'd be able to drive. He was going to be attending classes on blindness, though Collins swore his other eye was perfect. He might be having one more surgery before he came home. And he told her Zak was healing as well or better than expected.

Thank God for one little good piece of news.

With the list of medical treatment facilities Amy had to visit and register for, Collins had her busy running all over the county for the next two days. She had a stack of paperwork nearly a half-inch thick they would have to fill out. She wanted to wait until he returned from Germany—a project they could do together.

Four days after she returned to Coronado, Amy was dressed in one of her father's old tee shirts and an old pair of jeans while painting the bedroom in the apartment. Gina, Christy, and Shannon—T.J.'s. wife—stopped by without their kids. Gina looked like she was going to pop.

"I can't believe you haven't had that baby yet."

"Me, neither. Hoping Armando is home this week. You hear from Zak?"

"No." Amy took her brush to the kitchen sink.

"Love the mint green color," said Shannon. "You know the guys worry when they see us go into decorating mode. They think we're pregnant again."

"In your case, they'd be right," said Gina.

Christy gave Amy a hug, releasing her quickly. "How are you doing?"

"Good. Keeping busy."

"Anything we can get you? Do for you?"

"No, thanks, I'm good, Christy. Thanks for the offer. I'm just waiting until I get that call saying he's on American soil."

"We were going to grab a bite to eat. Thought we could convince you to come with us," said Shannon.

"Thanks, but I wanted to get this done. Then I can burn candles and keep the windows open to get rid of the paint smell before he comes home. I only have a couple of days."

"That's great news. He'll be home before the rest of the team, then."

"How come you didn't go visit him in Germany?" asked Shannon.

Amy went back to the kitchen and washed out her brush. "He hasn't called me, yet," she said to the bottom of the sink. "I think he's had more surgeries, according to Chief Collins. Talked to Kyle a couple of times, though, which I appreciate."

Amy didn't have to see their faces to understand the SEAL wives were sharing a look that transmitted 'something's not right.'

"You sure we can't do anything for you?" asked Gina again.

"I should be asking that to you, Gina. Sorry I've been a little distracted lately."

"I'm good. You would not believe how Armando's mother can't leave me alone. She even wanted to come today. She's so afraid I'll go into labor and she won't get to be right there beside me." Gina paused to rub her belly. "Ouch. This one is active. I think she just kicked my bladder."

"She? You're having a girl?" asked Amy.

"*I* think I'm having a girl. Armando thinks it's a boy, of course. That's all I do these days, just sit or sleep and wait. I'm too big to do anything else. We got the nursery set up before he left."

"So we rescued her," said Shannon. "And we made Felicia babysit."

Christy added, "Last chance for some recreational shopping. Or should I take a rain check on it?"

"Let's do that," said Amy. "I'm good. You guys go have fun."

She was standing in the front doorway, waving good-bye to her visitors, when Zak called her.

"Hi, Amy."

"Oh, Zak! It's wonderful to hear your voice." Her heart started to slam in her chest, and her cheeks blushed.

"I'm sorry I didn't call sooner." The monotone delivery scared her.

"Are you okay? How are you feeling?"

"Kyle told you how bad it is?"

"He told me about the conversations he'd had with your doctors, that's all. Why? How bad is it?" Amy hoped Zak didn't sense the lie.

"Bad."

She waited for him to say something.

"Well, I just wanted to let you know they're flying me home on Friday. Can you pick me up at the airport?"

"Of course, Zak. But how are you feeling, sweetheart?" She sensed she had to be cautious.

"It's complicated. I'll explain everything when I get back to San Diego."

'Get back to San Diego.' Not get back to me, to our home. Not come back to you. No 'Amy, I've missed you, Amy.'

"You don't sound like yourself, sweetheart. Maybe some good rest, walks on the beach, and some of our beautiful sun will be good for you."

"Hope so."

Not 'it will be nice to be home. Can't wait to see you.'

"I'll text you the details when I have them."

"Okay. Have you seen any of your guys?"

"Just Kyle and Alex. He got shot too. I think he's stateside already."

"He is. He's good."

The silence on Zak's end was making Amy wish she

hadn't mentioned running into Alex.

"I guess you'll be home a couple of days before the rest of them get here. Talked to Christy today." She was attempting to fill the space, keep him on the line, hoping to find a softening to his taught demeanor.

"That's good. Well, looks like I have to go now. See you Friday."

"Yes. I can hardly wait. Love you so much, Zak. I've missed you."

"It will be good to get back home. Bye."

It was what he wasn't saying that hurt the most. The emotional connection she had with him—that old-fashioned chemistry they were so good at—was still there. But it was hanging by a thread on his end. She didn't hear a single spark or reaction to anything in his voice. He also didn't mention how he was feeling. Did nothing to reassure her he was okay.

She sat down, the phone cradled in her lap as her tears softly fell. He'd called because he needed a ride from the airport.

Or maybe that was all he could muster to say.

She'd planned and organized, cleaned up, and prepared as best she knew how. In just two days, the real battle would begin.

CHAPTER 18

ZAK HELD HIS bandages, extra antibiotic wash, even his hospital toothbrush in a tan plastic drawstring baggie atop his duty bag. Hospital protocol required he be wheel-chaired out of the medical center, which annoyed him.

The morning session with the Navy shrink was a waste of time. He told the guy so, but got a mandatory series of sessions scheduled for him anyway. He had no say in the matter. As if he wasn't dealing with enough already, now he had to let them evaluate his mental state. Hell, most his buddies wouldn't pass that kind of scrutiny these days, especially after coming home from a firefight.

His new beard annoyed him too. The sunlight annoyed him. He was going home, and that annoyed him. And he was annoyed that he was annoyed.

The young Second Class Petty Officer tasked with getting him to the airport was chewing gum, and wearing silver wraparound shades, though the sky was cloudy, threatening rain. Zak judged he was probably his age, in his early twenties. He was a volunteer from the USO Warrior Center at Landstuhl.

"S.O. Chambers. Lookin' good. I'm Second Class Petty Officer Hayes, at your service," he said and then made a slight incantation of the head—not really a bow—to Zak. To the orderly, he smirked, "I got this." He wheeled the chair from the entrance ramp to the curb a few yards away where a dark blue VW Golf was parked. The orderly followed them.

"I can stand and walk on my own," insisted Zak when Hayes started to turn the chair around.

"Okay, you be the man, then."

Zak got up with ease. His leg wasn't hurting him any longer. His wrist and elbow were stiff from being immobilized. Zak had tossed the arm sling away on the trip down the hospital hallway.

The inside of the government-issue car smelled like some fake strawberry mixture. The scent was dangling from a MaiTai-shaped cardboard cutout hung on the rear view mirror. Zak found the young enlisted man irritatingly chipper.

"So where's home?"

"San Diego."

"Nice! That's not home; that's paradise."

The skin underneath his white bandage was beginning to itch again. He'd look for a back scratcher at the airport, but for now, he used his finger, slipping it up underneath the heavily padded wrap covering half his face and skull. He was going to let his beard continue to grow, but part of it was constricted by the bandage and tape, and that made him itch as well.

"What happened there?"

"I got shot."

"Oh Jeez, in the face?"

"Sort of." Zak leaned back so his good left eye could take in the young sailor.

"You over in Afghanistan or where?"

"That's classified. Sorry." Zak didn't want to tell him anyway.

"Oh. That's right. You're Special Ops."

THE AIRPORT COULDN'T come soon enough for Zak. He didn't want to be rude, but Hays was getting on his nerves big time, talking about how he loved German girls and all the great beer. Zak was helpless to endure the guy's tales of sexual exploits.

He thought about Amy. What would it be like to be close to her again? The thought of getting intimate with her filled him with dread. How long would she last if he had that attitude? He chastised himself for the fifth time today about this.

At the airport, Hayes handed the bag to another

USO representative who handed him his tickets and stayed with him until his connecting flight arrived.

As he walked down the airport halls, Zak was the object of much attention. They'd allowed him to fly in civilian clothes, but the presence of his helper in uniform identified him as a wounded vet. While the smiles and nods were well-meaning, Zak wanted to shrink into the ground and disappear. He hadn't had that much attention since his days on the high school football team. But unlike then, this attention made him feel like an invalid. A cripple.

After four transfers and nearly twenty hours, his plane touched down in San Diego. He was grateful for the shower he was able to get at the USO in Dallas before his last leg home. His seven-day beard remained. He fancied himself some kind of pirate, but instead of a sexy eye patch, he had this fuckin' white face obliterator. Alex was right. He could do a zombie movie, no problem.

He didn't have baggage, just the duty bag stuffed with things he'd brought to the Canaries. Absent the M4 and clips, his bag resembled the flesh hanging off an old horse. A muscled young man took the bag from him.

"Here, let me take that."

Zak clung to the bag until he saw the chocolate brown eyes of Alex. "Hey, man. Wow, didn't expect you." He checked the area around his Team buddy.

"Amy's with the car."

Zak wasn't sure why that bothered him, but it did. Amy said she had seen Alex. Were they now good friends? Talking on a regular basis? He was getting used to everything bothering him all the time now.

"Cool." He hoped his words masked the uneasiness he felt throughout his intestines. He'd had a stomach bordering on nausea the whole trip from Dallas.

"She invited me to come help her welcome you home. But if it was me, I'd rather have the little lady, all nekked and hot for my sorry ass being gone so long. Know what I'm sayin'?" He shrugged, waiting for a reaction from Zak.

The clean-shaven SEAL was the handsomest of the legendary bachelor SEALs. He'd gotten some sun, and he appeared healthier than he'd last seen him. Zak knew his own picture resembled one of the Iranian hostages he'd seen on TV years ago. He was the guy with the big white bandage on his face. That guy had a beard and only one eye showing, too.

Alex watched him do the head thing. Thinking about everything—anything—but getting intimate with Amy. Maybe he knew that, Zak thought. Maybe he thought he could slip in there when he wasn't around? Maybe Amy had formed a quickie friendship with him.

"You help her ease the pain, my friend?" His words

sounded bitter. Not at all the way he needed to talk to his team.

"Fuck no. That's not me, man. Maybe some regular Navy grunt, but not me."

So now he'd managed to piss off Alex too, and all he'd wanted to do was help out. Or that's what he said.

Who knew the truth?

Am I jealous? Or am I just angry? He was probably making it all up, but his frustration was focusing on Alex at that moment as if all the things about his situation had been stolen by him, not by circumstance. He'd stepped up to the plate and been a hero, and now his life would be shit forever.

The thoughts rattled around and around in his head until he felt Alex grab his cheeks, slap them with his hands, and yell for God and everyone on the planet to hear, "Fuck sake, Zak. You're alive! You're fuckin' back in the U.S. of A."

Zak delivered Alex a murderous glare just as the people behind him gathered in a polite semicircle—complete strangers—and began to clap.

If there wasn't a crowd of troop supporters around to witness it, Zak would have punched Alex out right then and there. He'd have knocked two teeth out of his fuckin' head, too.

Obligation and duty forced him to turn and give a grin to the crowd, waving, but inside, it felt like a grimace.

"They love you, man," Alex said, his arms out-stretched.

Zak had started for the exit. Alex ran to catch up to him. Zak stopped, and the two of them nearly collided. He narrowed his eyes and focused on Alex's Adam's apple, the place he wanted to punch so badly it was making his knuckles sore just from the thought of it. "You do that again, Alex, and I'll fuckin' kill you."

Amy's frame was small behind the wheel of the huge maroon hummer. She struggled with the big door and then ran around the front of the truck. He could tell she was forcing herself not to notice the bandage.

She stopped herself right before she reached him. Taking the last step deliberately eyes raking over his chest, she then laid her cheek on his sternum. "Welcome home, Zak." He could feel the vibration of her torso as she spoke the words in a low growl.

The sensation of holding her was overwhelming. His hands found the back of her waist, following up the trail her spine made, until one hand massaged the back of her neck. It was an instinctive gesture. Something he didn't have to think about.

She was trembling. Before the deployment, he'd have reassured her he was present and nothing could hurt her, beg her to be strong, not to be afraid. But he couldn't go that far today. As if she was poison to him, he suddenly released her and took a step back.

"Oh, I'm sorry. Does it hurt?"

He saw her little lapse, her eyes shifting for a millisecond over his face covering, checking it out. She recovered quickly, her eyes riveted on him again.

He felt like a complete heel. The sight of her sweet face and luscious body frightened him more than he'd imagined. "Just a little."

"Come on, lovebirds. Let's get you home." Alex threw the bag in the front seat, opened up the rear door, and motioned for them to crawl in.

Amy's smooth ass preceded him as she climbed up into the second seat. In the old days, he would have told her how much he'd dreamt of that ass, of what she meant to him, of how her body set him on fire.

But letting those feelings anywhere close to him right now was the scariest thing he'd ever done in his life. He was suddenly sitting next to the one person in the whole world who terrified him—not for who she was, but for who *he* had become.

CHAPTER 19

AMY'S HEART WAS racing as she bounced in the back seat of the Hummer. Alex had a country station on, a little loud. She figured he'd wanted to give them privacy, but it was hard to hear each other without shouting.

Her thigh rested against his. His bandage wasn't as prominent when she sat on his left, as she was now. She felt the heat of his body the entire length of hers. The beard made him seem older. She snuck little glances at his profile when he turned to the right, glancing away in time not to be caught.

She gently grabbed one of his hands, holding it with both of hers. She traced an imaginary line with her forefinger up and down his fingers, one by one, and around his palm. He gazed down, expressionless.

She brought his palm to her cheek and turned to him. His body flinched. Even though she was the one pressing his hand against her, the touch of her man still brightened her spirit. Zak was inside there, somewhere, she thought as she watched his brow furrow slightly and then the lines disappear. He gave no further indication of what was going on with him, and she made the decision not to press.

"I'm so glad you're home, Zak," she whispered. She doubted he could hear but noticed he'd paid attention to her lips moving and knew what she said anyway.

His eyes slowly closed. When he opened them, there was moisture there.

"I'm sorry," he mouthed.

He removed his hand and brought his arm around her, resting partially on the back seat. Amy relished the feel of his quiet strength. She wanted to snuggle under the weight of his huge shoulder, but sensed he didn't want that.

At the apartment, Alex was going to bring the bag to Zak's front door.

"No way, man. This is fine. You've done more than enough. Thanks," Zak said as the two SEALs hugged briefly.

"Now, you guys have fun tonight," Alex said, winking at Amy.

"Thanks for coming. I appreciate it," she whispered.

"Sure thing, doll." He leaned over, giving her a kiss on the cheek, and left.

At the front door, Amy produced her key and unlocked their apartment. She stepped to the side so Zak could see what she'd done to make it more attractive.

He dropped the black satchel and scanned the walls. Amy had purchased a few large plants, including a tree fern that nearly touched the ceiling. She'd covered the living room couch with a green pastel quilt she'd bought in a second hand store and found pillows to match. She moved the weight set that had been in the living room and Zak's desk to the second bedroom. A framed print of the ocean in pastels hung over the couch, blending with the green walls and white ceiling.

There was still a bit of a paint smell, but the place was clean and dotted with area rugs and colorful accessories. She'd milk painted the coffee table a light salmon. The back of the pantry door in the kitchen, she'd painted over with chalkboard paint. *Welcome Home, Zak* was written in green chalk with a red heart drawn underneath it. She'd placed yellow roses both on the kitchen counter and the dinette table.

"You went to a lot of work, Amy. Looks nice."

"You like it?"

"Doesn't resemble anything it did before." He gave her a half-smile. "You did all this for me?"

"Of course. I did it for us. I wanted our first night together here to be special, Zak." She walked to him. His arms remained at his sides at first as she pressed against him, balancing her forearms on his shoulders. "I'm so glad you're home, sweetheart."

She kissed him and then felt the familiar sensation of his hands rubbing over her backside, up her back, finally pulling her to him, his erection pressing against her lower belly. Their kiss deepened, and although Amy tried to avoid the bandage, her nose rubbed against the white cotton. Her hair brushed over the adhesive tape. As they parted, the familiar way her heart slammed against her insides filled her with delicious fantasies. Something was pulling at her hair when she noticed several strands were caught in the tape. She used her fingers to remove the rest of it from the stubborn adhesive.

"Sorry, I'm not used to it yet. I'm sure in time—"

"You better get used to it. Going to need several surgeries. This will be me for the foreseeable future." He stepped back, his head bobbing, hand splayed at the top of his chest.

"No worries, Zak. I'll get used to it. I just have to learn. That's all."

Zak turned around. Not wanting any space between them, Amy spooned behind him, feeling him stiffen as her palms called to him, begging to explore his chiseled abs, one by one. She lifted his shirt and kissed his bare skin down low, kissed up his spine until she was pulling his shirt over his head, dropping it to the side. She removed her top and unclasped her bra, letting him feel the warmth of her breasts against his back while her palms pulled him hard against her. "God, Zak, I've missed you so much."

Her hands migrated lower to cover his cock, and she stroked the length of it through his jeans. His hands were on hers immediately, stopping her.

"What is it, honey?"

"I can't do this, Amy."

She stepped in front of him. He glanced down briefly at her tits, her engorged nipples feeling hot and needing release. "Why? What's wrong, Zak?"

"Can't you see? Are you completely blind?"

"Of course not." Her hand migrated to touch the bandage, and he stopped her.

"No."

"It doesn't make any difference to me." She reached for his groin again, and again, his hands stopped her. The way he held her wrists was a little too forceful and hurt.

"Don't."

"What is it, Zak? Tell me."

"I don't feel like it anymore. I just—this is just too close for me right now."

"But, sweetheart, you've gone through an ordeal. Let me soften it. Let me love you, Zak. Please." Her fingers lightly traveled over his forearms to his nipples and then in a slow arc downward. Two fingers on her right hand tried to find space inside the front of his jeans at the waistband.

"I said no!" His command scared her.

Amy found one of the used overstuffed chairs she'd bought and sat down, crossing her legs. She let her blouse drape open. He was turned away from her. From the back and side of him, no one would be able to tell he had a bandage on his face. Silent tears dripped down onto her chest, over her breasts, and onto her lap. "Sit down and let's talk then."

"I don't want to fuckin' talk."

"So what am I supposed to do, Zak?"

He faced her again. "I seriously think I should leave."

"Not a chance."

"I need some time, Amy." His shoulders drooped, arms hanging at the sides. His fingers nervously flexed and released as his head angled back and to the right. She saw that he was in a huge amount of emotional pain. "Don't push. I'm not very good company."

"You can take all the time you need." She wiped the tears from her face with the backs of her hands. His expression changed.

"I'm sorry."

"No, I think I'm sorry, Zak. I guess I should have known when you didn't call me there was something going on." Amy carefully, slowly buttoned up her shirt and, without looking at him, stood up. She picked up her bra from the floor. "Come on. I'll show you the office I made for you. And I think you'll like the way I fixed up our bedroom."

Amy put one foot in front of the other, numbed by the interaction, which wasn't anything like what she expected. She heard his movements behind her, following. Turning the door handle to the office, she pushed it open and let him peer inside.

"Big improvement. Thank you."

Amy still didn't turn to scan his face, continuing down to the master bedroom with the door open. She'd placed candles all around the bed and on the dressers she'd painted and distressed with muted Caribbean colors of turquoise and light rose.

The beautiful stage had been set, but there were no actors in this passion play. The king-sized bed lay idle. She knew it was selfishness that was burrowing a hole in her gut.

"I'm very grateful to be home. Thank you for all of this. Give me a little time, but don't expect too much at first, okay?"

When she faced him, studying the custom fit partial mask he wore, she needed to tell him the truth.

"Okay, Zak. I promise to give you that time. Take all you need. I'm not going anywhere. This is our home now. You're here, but you're not. You come back to me, and I'll wait. Just don't take too long."

AMY PUT HER nightgown on and slipped into bed, her back to Zak's side. She heard the shower running and smelled the clean fresh scent of soap as it bubbled over his body.

It had been a full day, ripe with anticipation. But like so many things in life, she never could have predicted this. She let her tears flow, careful with her breathing so he wouldn't hear her. Her heart was cracked open and lay bleeding. Surrounded by a community she knew cared about her, a loving father, and a husband now back from a difficult trip overseas, injured both physically and mentally, she just couldn't shake the feeling that she was all alone. Amy knew this would be the first of many such dark days. Zak was a different man, not the man who left. And maybe that Zak, the old Zak she'd fallen in love with, maybe he would never return. That sobering thought stopped her tears as fear gripped her.

And then she remembered her promise. "I'll always be here when you come home." That meant being here for whenever and whatever she would face. That's what she'd signed on to.

Zak's side of the bed dented as she heard his massive body slide into the sheets. She felt his hand on her hip, heard his whisper in her ear, and it made her ears buzz.

"I'm really sorry, honey." He patted her hip. "I don't want you to see me yet. I sleep with the bandage off. When morning comes, please let me get up first. Promise?"

"I promise," she said through her tears.

CHAPTER 20

THE EARLY MORNING hours of each day was turning out to be a time Zak would lie in bed, watch the designs on the ceiling, and think. In the hospital, it was never completely quiet, even during these hours, so he guessed that's why he was waking up then.

This morning, he was in his old bedroom, lying next to Amy, now his wife, who was soundly sleeping after crying herself to sleep again. It was becoming a routine, and not one he enjoyed. It had kept him up, listening to her attempts to stifle evidence of her pain. There was still something left of his desire to protect her, but he wrote it off. His hand on her hip could have easily turned into something else. That something else was making him hard in spite of all his confusion.

Now, except for the gentle sounds of her slumber, the room was quiet.

His fingers came up to his face, the injured part. He'd tried to roll over on his left, but this morning, just as most other mornings in the hospital, he'd woken up on his back. The ridges of the train track designs of stitches, especially the ones under his eye, itched, but did not pucker as they had before. His body was well on its way to smoothing over the rough edges of this invasion to his flesh. What the final result would be was still uncertain. His new doctors at the clinic would have some opinions on that when he saw them next week for the follow-up.

Aware he was pushing the interaction with Amy forcefully out of his head, he opened the door a bit to explore why that was. He was practicing for his next appointment with the shrink.

The shrink the Navy had assigned asked him about intimacy. His answer at the time was, "Why, do I wear a sign that says 'doesn't like to screw anymore'?"

"You think intimacy is screwing?" the doctor questioned.

"Our intimacy always wound up with screwing. I'd say we were *overscrewers*, if you want to know the truth. Sort of like over-achievers? Is that a term for your little book?" Zak pointed to the doctor's spiral notebook.

"This isn't about me or my little book. It's about you, and examine these things. Maybe you're not ready. Is that what you're saying?"

"Ready for sex? I'm always ready for sex, doc."

The doctor removed his glasses, leaned forward on his desk placing his palms down with his middle fingers touching. "I know you SOF guys are tough. I know you see a lot of things you shouldn't have to see out there, and do stuff—"

"Doc." Zak stood up. "Let me save you some time. I've been trained as a SEAL. My very first mission was less than a week old and this happened. The only horrible thing I experienced was this." He pointed to his head. "Don't they give you guys our files? How can you help someone when you don't know anything about them?"

The doctor stood slowly. "Well, that was going to be your job, son."

"Don't call me son. I'm not your fuckin' son."

"No. And I'll bet your father isn't very proud of you. I do know you have a father who has been a borderline alcoholic, which seemed to rub off on you as well. If the Navy is your last chance at redemption, you're doing a shitty job of treating it like the gift it is." He sat down and wrote notes in his book.

Zak didn't know how to process it. He turned to go and heard the doctor's irritated voice shouting behind him, "You will be here next week, same time. Maybe then you can leave your fucked up self in the car and bring the real SEAL, the man who wears his Trident proudly, maybe you can bring that guy here. We'll talk.

Have a nice day, Zak."

He'd picked a fight with just about everyone that day and felt ashamed.

Why am I doing this to myself? To Amy? It isn't anyone's fault, so why am I so angry?

He knew he loved her. He just couldn't show it, and that puzzled him. It was as if he was under some kind of deep freeze, making him incapable of showing the affection he knew he had deep down inside. He didn't want to hurt her, but that part of showing affection in return for hers was turned off. He should be making more of an effort. He decided he'd try harder.

What are you afraid of? The doctor had asked him that.

There was something out there, standing in the shadows, but he couldn't get the figure to step into the circle of light. So many things were lurking just outside his ability to experience them.

She was still asleep when she rolled over and pulled herself close to him, just like she used to do. He allowed the back of his hand to rub up and down her upper arm where she'd tucked herself into a warm cocoon beside him. The touch of her flesh against his automatically aroused him.

At least that part is still working.

He wondered if having sex with her would make her feel better. Never mind what he would feel. Would it help her? Or was it taking advantage of her to do this when his barren insides didn't allow him to fully engage? He didn't want to use her for his needs. That wouldn't be right, or honorable. Just why couldn't he *feel* that love he once had for her? Did they remove a part of his brain when they stitched him up? Was that it? He'd have to ask the doctors.

She was waking up, the result of his carelessness in stroking the side of her arm, his little signal he wanted the encounter he was afraid to ask for in the light of day. He felt her body heat rise as she unfolded herself, as she began kissing his chest in the dark, thanks to the merciful blackout curtains.

She was clutching his balls underneath his pajama bottoms, stroking his shaft, allowing a tiny moan to emit from the depths of her need. He anticipated what her lips would feel like on him. Should he let her? Was this for her or for him that he was letting her move on him, slip down the barrier between their bodies, search with her tongue, suck him hard, and pull on his ball sack. She wrapped her legs around his right thigh, pressing her mound against him. Her needy moan vibrated everything.

His hand went to her face he could not see, feeling the indentation in her cheeks as she sucked, feeling the soft folds of the underside of her chin. He needed the darkness so she wouldn't see who he really was.

His hardness was nearly painful as she worked on him. He held her head, palms over her ears, pushing and pulling it up and down on him, each stroke making him longer and harder.

He heard her gasp as she pressed her pubic bone against him with such force it almost hurt his previously injured leg. It was like she could feel his pain somehow. She was in pain, too. She needed him. Scary things were in the hallways of his mind as he walked toward sexual satisfaction. Love was here somewhere, but not now, not in the selfish need of his flesh.

Was this wrong?

"Zak, make love to me. Please make love to me," she was mewing, begging him.

Could he do this? *Am I taking advantage?* He couldn't make up his mind. She was climbing on top of him, and her fingers squeezed his nipple while she bit his other one. She was a woman in need, without shame, on a collision course with desire.

Her fingers covered his lips and then slid under his chin, up his neck, and into his hairline. He stopped her hand before she could reach any of the scaring on his scalp, or what had been replaced as his scalp.

"Zak, please. Make love to me," she said as she drew one leg over his, as she dragged the lips of her sex over him, grinding and attempting to mate wherever she could find purchase.

He could not let her see him. She'd be horrified, even though right now that was probably not anything she was thinking about. He needed to keep the illusion he was whole.

His cock was demanding action, and this angered him. Surprised, he blamed her for his need. If she hadn't aroused him, he wouldn't have that need. But she was telling him—no, showing him—he was not a eunuch. His sexual desires had nothing to do with everything else going on inside him. His body wanted to have sex with her, even if he couldn't grapple with the emotional side of it.

Is this taking advantage?

He should stop her.

"Zak, you're hurting me," she said. His hands had taken hold of her wrists, holding them away from his body, even as her lower body arched and caressed into his.

He was going to get up and go fix himself in the shower, do something to take care of the need. The warm water would blank out everything else as he gave himself to oblivion, took care of his bodily needs.

But suddenly, reflex pushed her down onto the bed on her back. Then he flipped her to her side, urgently lifting her nightie from her behind as she writhed, moved against him, and moaned every time he touched her ass. Zak slipped an arm under her chest and pulled her shoulder down so she was slammed tight against him. Amy had gone molten, her movements fluid. Her sweet ass pressed into his groin, spreading her knees, making herself available to him, using her hands to come to a tripod. His wife arched then slipped her leg outside of his. Her sex was right there, wet and pulsing as he pressed a thumb inside her. He heard the delicious inhale, which spurred him on, his cock seeking the root it needed.

Pulling his pillow from behind him, he jammed it under her pelvis, elevating her sex between that tight little package. Her arousal was intoxicating. Hungry for the taste of her, his hands spread her cheeks wide as he plundered her with his tongue, sucking the juices she was pressing into his mouth.

Amy came up on her knees, and he followed her. She pushed down her own pillow beneath, preparing her angle, begging for penetration.

He could barely see in the early dawn breaking. His world was focused on the slippery feel of the crevice between her butt cheeks as his cock traveled up and down, rubbing his crown against her clit and pressing against her folds. Zak found himself snagged on her entrance, and he stopped. Amy groaned, moved toward him, and he held himself back. She moved again, raising her pelvis, finding his cock, and matching it with her channel. One finger rimmed her opening slowly, guiding his way. With his right hand, he reached underneath her and squeezed her clit as he rammed himself deep inside her.

Amy's moan told him she was ruined. He pushed inside deeper still, grabbing her hips so he could ride her hard. The slapping of their thighs against each other punctuated her little mewling sounds when he slowed, allowing his long, hard thrusts and holds. He angled his hips to the right and then left before beginning the fierce pumping action again. Then he slowed down to hear her breathing, to feel her shuddering beneath him.

Her muscles clamped down on him. She pushed herself up on her arms, arching her back as his hands held her at the hips, moving her against him as he drilled her.

She hissed as he felt the spasms overtake her. He wanted her to explode beneath him. Zak pushed harder, deeper, until he began to feel his release coming. His hands pulled her hips, jamming her body into him as he filled her, let her feel his lurching cock. He held his breath as he pumped into her one last time, allowing her to milk him to the finish line.

Her round ass shone in the early dawn light. The streaks of sweat traveled down her spine. His own torso was wet. Sweat poured off his forehead, dripping down his nose and over his lips. Still deep inside her as her muscles began to relax, he leaned back to see the point of their joining. Slipping his cock out, he replaced it with two fingers, and Amy groaned into the mattress. He rubbed her lips, her little stiff bud as she jumped beneath him, making sure she was fully spent.

She was trying to roll over to face him. He kept his head turned to the right while lifting her up and placing her against him, spooned into the bed on her side. He pressed his forehead against her shoulders as their breathing labored. He opened his mouth to say something, but couldn't find the words. Her fingers lightly smoothed over his left thigh.

"Love you, Zak."

It took everything he had, but he returned with, "Love you, Amy. Thank you for—"

What? Thank you for letting me use you?

Through his guilt and remorse, the shame of his need, he found the honest words at last. "Thank you for loving me. I'll give you what I can. I'm not sure it will be enough."

Like Cinderella, his midnight was coming. The light in the room would make his face fully visible to her soon, which meant he had to go back to the protection of his bandage, hide behind the white cotton device that kept the rest of the world out.

"Don't turn around. Stay here," he whispered in her ear.

On the bathroom counter, he lifted the white form toward his face. He stopped to examine himself. He could see a tiny portion of his eye underneath the dark swelling of his upper lid. It was red and nasty looking with a yellowish discharge coming from his tear duct. Most of the redness was gone underneath the stitching, as well as some of the lumps and bumps. He touched his cheek, letting his fingers travel over the surface, his eyes closed. No, it was not smooth. It might never be smooth. At his scalp, little dark tufts of hair had started growing like weeds in a crack in the sidewalk.

He placed the cotton form over his face and re-applied tape to hold it in place.

Let her imagine what's underneath. Whatever she could imagine, it will be even worse to her.

And then he wondered if he could keep it private forever.

CHAPTER 21

AMY PLANNED TO go with Zak to his string of appointments stretching over the next several days. The thaw that had started his first night back stalled, like an icebreaker ship caught between shelves of ice in the artic sea. She remembered seeing it on an adventure channel. The crew had to wait until a bright day with full sunlight to give the ice a little help so the ship could crash its way through.

That's how she felt about Zak right now. He was a big, complicated iceberg. Quiet—and there wasn't anything unusual about that—but without the little things he used to do, like slip her hair behind her ear, whisper how sexy she looked, slide behind her in bed, touch her in places that made her thighs tremble. She was on pins and needles.

Instead, they were like two strangers passing in a crowded room, trying to avoid touching one another. She stopped reaching out for him, trying to hug him or take his hand. Every time she did, he flinched in reaction. She wasn't sure anymore whether she stopped because she didn't think he liked it or because she felt so bad he reacted so negatively. Was he suddenly repulsed by her now that they'd had sex? Did she make some mistake showing him how much she missed him? Her heart told her it wasn't a mistake. That she should continue to try.

Kyle and the others on Team 3 arrived the following week. Zak insisted on waiting out front for the boys to pick him up one evening. When they returned him home, he'd been drinking, which was the first time since his accident, since before they got married.

He wasn't gentle with her that night as he groped her in his drunken state, flipped her over on her stomach, and pumped her from behind. Without the foreplay and the long languid kisses afterwards, the whole sex act was over in less than five minutes. She got up immediately afterwards and took a shower, washing the beer breath and dirty sex sweat from her body, her sobs hidden by the sound of the water.

When she came back to bed, he was asleep. He'd pulled his pillow over his head, but the snoring was barely muffled. The white bandage lay on the carpet beside the bed. She wanted to take it and burn it as if it was responsible for the monster her husband had become.

In the morning, he apologized and, with his bandage in place, drew her near, holding her but not moving them into another encounter. Amy told herself at least he'd apologized and tabled the discussion on this horrible behavior for another day.

But every time she thought about it, tears brimmed over onto her cheeks. There was the comparison always rolling around her brain between the beautiful long attentive sex her husband gave her so passionately before he left, to this man who came home to her. She did not know this man, and he scared her.

He smelled the same. His breathing sounded the same as she laid her ear against his chest. The magic of his touch was still there, whether or not it was actually his or something she was creating because of their now distant connection. Everything was the same, and yet it was all different. He was only half present, like some weaker version of himself was all he would show. It was hard not to miss the man he had been and to accept this one in his place. But she began to fear this might be what the rest of her life would look like.

AMY WAS SEATED behind the curtained screen in the eye examining room. She heard the doctor speak to him after he'd made his first examination. "Your eye is angry right now, Zak. I'm glad the swelling is down, and it appears the pressure is, too. I can't get an accurate reading without anesthetizing you, though. That eyelid is nasty."

"I'm seeing little flashes of light, I think. Maybe its just memory, though," Zak mumbled.

Amy sat up straight, taking hope. She wanted to say something encouraging, but bit her lip.

Why didn't he tell me this?

"That's good, but I don't think it's a real image. It could be your nerve regenerating a bit, like an engine sputtering to life. Not enough to carry the whole train, but enough to belch and bellow. We'll have to monitor that."

She could see light through the curtain, the angle of Zak's head tilted back, held in place by a chin rest. The beam moved back and forth quickly.

"You see anything?"

"Don't think so."

"Close your other eye tight." After more manipulation, he asked again, "Anything now?"

"No, sir, but it hurts when you flash it in there."

"Hmmm. You might be having some sensation then. I'll take that as a good sign."

Amy heard Zak ask him if he could put the bandage back on.

"Yes, son. You do that."

The curtain was withdrawn, and Zak stood towering over the doctor.

"You're healthy and strong, son. If there were any way this eye was going to by some miracle regenerate, it would be to a young man like you. But—" He held his forefinger up, frown lines developing on his forehead. His eyebrows knotted beneath the bridge on his glasses. "—Not a promise. We're doing everything possible. It's up to the body to do what the body does. Think positive, but please, son, be prepared for the worst." He slid his glasses down on his nose, looking over them to Amy. "That goes for you, too, little lady."

Zak nodded, glanced over at her, and gave her a tiny arch at the left side of his mouth, a smile trying to be born.

"She's got the optimism, doc. I'm a realist, and I don't expect much anymore."

The smile was gone. The doctor was taken aback. Amy could see worry pass over his face as Zak picked up his paperwork and headed to the door.

Amy walked up to the physician. "What are the odds?"

"Have you not seen his face?"

"No. He's—"

"Amy?" Zak said, returning from around the corner. "You ready?"

THEY MET WITH Zak's physical therapist the next day, who examined his arm and thigh, moving them to check the range of motion in his elbow, shoulder, hip, and knee. She took notes on a clipboard and then informed him the bone repair was healing well, but that he would have a half-inch difference between his two leg lengths. She tested his reaction to pinprick on the soles of his feet. Stripped down to his boxers with no shirt, she watched him walk toward and away from her and continued to make notes. She had him bend over to try to touch his toes.

She had him balance on one leg and he nearly collapsed.

Her demeanor was gentle with Zak. "So I'm going to recommend no more jumping out of airplanes for now at least."

Amy saw a smile finally grace his lips. The therapist winked at her and threw his clothes at him. Zak barely caught them in time.

"Good reflexes."

"Yes, ma'am." He was smiling again. Amy prayed it was evidence of a beginning thaw.

"I'm going to have you do some stretching exercises. Nothing too strenuous for now. Definitely no running, Zak. Nothing to upset that eye and your soft tissue healing, okay?"

He nodded.

"Here come some questions you're not going to enjoy answering, but then, there's always one—but I don't think you're that kind." She had her arms crossed across her large chest. With her slim waist and hips, Amy thought she looked like a fifty-year-old Barbie doll. Her blonde hair was still long, braided and crossing her head like a crown. She wore a silk flower clip at her right temple.

"Ready?" Her eyebrows rose.

"Yes, ma'am."

"Well, get dressed and then have a seat."

Zak obeyed, slipping his jeans up over his boxers. His abs flexed as he carefully put his tee shirt over his head and pulled it down. The therapist was making notes in her chart and didn't notice. Zak sat next to Amy, and they both waited for her questions.

"First, how's your elimination?"

"Excuse me?"

"Your poop and pee?"

Zak made a face, most of it obscured by the bandage, and shrugged. "Fine. No issues."

"Good. And how about your sex life?"

"What do—what exactly are you asking?"

"Do you guys fuck regularly?" She removed her bright blue glasses and chewed on one earpiece.

Amy froze in place. Her urge to protect him trumped any concern for his embarrassment. "He just got back. He's been tired." She turned to look for agreement from him and was greeted with an evil eye.

One. Evil. Eye.

Zak's frustration showed in his heavy exhales. "Pam, can I call you Pam?"

"You may."

"We're working on that. As far as whether my plumbing works, it works fine, and yes, we've tested it. But I'm still getting used to the fact that anything like that we do has to be done in the complete dark. For obvious reasons."

Their eyes locked until the therapist nodded slightly and then glanced over at Amy.

"But nothing hurts, right?"

"No," he answered, staring down at his hands.

Pam was watching her carefully. The unspoken answer Amy gave her was, *'Only my heart.'*

ON THE WAY home, Amy couldn't help the tears from cascading down her cheeks.

"Come on. Don't start that again."

She could barely speak. "I've been trying to be strong."

"You can hardly look at me without crying. I'm reminded about who I am not every time I see your face."

"Zak, that's not fair. I'm trying to be sensitive. I've been careful. I try not to disturb you. I cook for you, clean for you. I've gotten all this paperwork you'll need for your medical treatment, and it's just sitting there on the table, waiting for you to complete it. I go with you to your appointments and—"

"I think that's a bad idea. If you're going to have private conversations with my doctors, do it so I don't know about it."

"What are you talking about?"

"The optometrist. You were discussing something in private with him, or trying to."

"I asked him what he thought your chances were you would see again from that eye." She brushed away her tears. "And then he asked me if I'd seen your face."

"And you told him no?"

"I told him the truth."

Zak didn't say a word all the way home. When they pulled up to the apartment complex, after shutting off the truck, he sat with his hands on the steering wheel. Leaves blew over the windshield, dancing in a late summer wind, reminding her that summer was gone. A lot of things were gone. It was about to become winter in San Diego, which wasn't much of a weather change, but it would still be winter. For a lot of reasons.

"Maybe we need to have that talk. You know what talk that is, Amy, don't you?"

"No. I'm not sure what you mean anymore. Please spell it out for me. I feel like I don't know—"

"Oh, stop it. Quit complaining." His fists hit the

steering wheel. "Fuck!" he shouted, which made her jump.

"Quit complaining? How dare you say that? I've not complained at all since you've been back."

"You cry every time you see me. I catch you watching me when you don't think I do."

"That's not complaining, Zak. I used to do that before too, or don't you remember?"

"Ah, no use. There's just no fuckin' way we can talk about this."

"What is it, Zak? What is it that you cannot tell me? I'm here for you. For the long haul. I've said it so many times, I get the impression you don't hear it anymore."

"We should go inside to have this conversation."

That suited her just fine. Anger was percolating in her belly. When she slipped down off the bench seat, her spine was jarred when her feet hit the ground. She slammed the door so hard even Zak turned toward her in alarm.

She hoisted her purse over her shoulder and walked fast, slightly ahead of him, all the way to the front door of their apartment. Just inside the door, she dropped her bag and slipped off her shoes. She made a big glass of ice water for herself without asking Zak if he wanted one, just made one for him and shoved it in his chest, practically pushing him backward with the force of it.

She plopped down on the overstuffed chair. "You

asked me to give you time. It's been three weeks, Zak. Not an eternity, but it's about time we start moving in one direction or the other."

He sat tentatively on the couch opposite her, crossing his legs, sipping on the water, his other arm extended down over the top of the padded fabric. "So tell me what those directions are again, Amy?"

"Have I done something to offend you?"

"No."

"Is it me? Are you tired of me?"

"How could it be you?"

"You don't want to touch me. You don't give me any encouragement at all. You fuck like I'm some piece of meat. Zak, where does all that come from? This was never you before. What's changed?"

"I don't want to make you spend your life with me, a freak, a cripple, someone you have to feel sorry for all the time. I want to stop saying I'm sorry, not because it isn't the right thing to do, but because I don't hurt you anymore."

"Except that you are hurting me. You are hurting me every day, every hour we're together."

"Fuck that, Amy. You're not the one with the face of a Cyclops. How could you even compare your pain to mine?"

"Shut up, Zak." Amy stood and started for the hallway to go cry herself to sleep on the bed.

"Oh I see. Quitting now, are we?"

She wanted to slap him. "You are a monster! Not for how ugly you must be now, your face, your healing flesh. You're a monster because of what's inside you." She regretted saying it, but the force of her rage wasn't giving up easily. Even deep breaths didn't help today.

"Sit down. Let's finish this," Zak said tersely.

"Okay, let's." Amy allowed her defiant tone to infect the poison of their already nasty conversation. Never had it been this way, even when they'd disagreed before. She knew he wanted to hurt her, emotionally hurt her.

"You want out, you get out. We get an annulment, and we're done. You can go screw all the guys up on the Police Force if you like to. Just don't come show your face around here anymore. If that's your choice, let's just be done with it and move on."

Amy couldn't sit. With her arms crossed, she shouted, "Asshole."

He was focusing on magazines on the table.

"Look at me, or are you a coward, Zak?"

He squinted and finally did return her gaze.

"I have about as much interest in the guys in Santa Rosa as you do fucking sheep. Don't you ever say that to me again. I'm not a fuckin' quitter, Zak. Just because you are, don't make the mistake of calling me one. You owe me that, and I don't give a flying fuck if you like it or not."

He was silent. Something had shifted. She saw him stifle a snicker.

"I'll give you this, Amy, you're damn sexy when you swear. Man, you've picked up some choice ones while I've been gone." He shook his head, arms crossed over themselves, but his gaze was fixed on the magazines.

Amy was still angry, but his comment caught her up short. In spite of everything that had been said, she wanted to go over to him, kneel, and beg that Zak she still hoped was inside to come out. But she knew it would be the wrong thing to do. She realized they needed help to untangle the knots that had formed. "Maybe we need to go through counseling. Christy said a lot of the guys go to Dr. Brownlee or Libby, Coop's wife—"

"Not Libby! And not that fuckin' shrink the Navy sent me to."

"Okay, so Dr. Brownlee, then. I just can't continue feeling like I'll do something really wrong and you'll flash out of here, maybe even hurt me. Can you answer that, Zak? Am I in danger? I want the truth."

"I would never hurt you, Amy. You should know that by now."

She sucked in air because she had to tell him fair and square. "How would I know that, Zak? You already have. But I'd gladly bear it, if I felt there was some improvement, some end in sight to this nightmare."

"Did you ever consider perhaps we shouldn't be together now? I have all this rehab and issues with the Navy wanting to retire me out. I've had one of the shortest fuckin' careers as a SEAL in the history of the teams. I spent more time in training—nearly two years preparing and then trying out and then training more—than I ever did on deployment."

"So you deal with all these things. We deal with all these things together. Unless, as you say, you feel we shouldn't be together. Is that what you're saying? Because I haven't changed my mind about you. Have you changed your mind about me? Am I suddenly not worthy now? You don't think I can handle it? Is that what all this is about? Do I have to suffer some huge life-changing injury before you'll accept me? Is my sacrifice not worthy?"

She worried she had gone too far. Right now, he wasn't quick to anger, thank God. He was quick to frustration, though. But not anger.

"I don't want to have you treat me like a convalescing child."

"But you *are* convalescing. You going to deny that? You could lose your eye if you aren't careful. When are you going to face, really face, the reality of where you're at, Zak? It's not going away."

"When are you going to face who you've gotten yourself stuck with?"

"Stuck with? You think I see you that way, Zak? I love you. I've always loved you. What could possibly change that? You mean some ugly bandage and some scarring and a bloodshot eye? That what you're saying? Because that won't do it. I want you back. I want all of you. Every part of you!"

"You want this?"

Zak ripped off his bandage. The face that grimaced back at her, full of pain, full of self pity, reminded her of a lost and injured puppy left at the side of a busy road, alone, shuddering, not knowing where to run to safety.

She knew her face registered shock. She blinked, not believing what she was seeing. Gasping for air, her mouth dry, the adrenaline pumping throughout her veins—it would have been easier to turn away, but she wouldn't. She couldn't give up on him. It didn't *look* like him, but she'd find him.

Somehow she'd find him.

CHAPTER 22

SO THERE IT was. Evidence she couldn't hardly stand to look at him. He had to see it. It was the completion of the injury that had happened at the Canaries. This wound came last—the face of the woman he'd have died for, would still die for—repulsed and scared out of her wits. He could see it was going to be hard on her. It would require everything she had.

He could make nice. That would be the gentlemanly thing to do, and in his former world, that's what he would have tried to do: be gracious. But it had to be done this way. She needed to decide if it was cut and run or stay. And if she stayed, she wouldn't be allowed to pity him, or he'd leave.

He was glad the stirrings he'd been having about the regret for his actions since coming home weren't fully intact. Otherwise, this would be even more painful than it was. No, this was her time to decide. He wouldn't influence her one iota. It might appear like he didn't care, but he did. He was afraid of himself he cared so much. Maybe tonight that scab would be picked and it would be all over.

Whatever it was, she wanted real. Well, real was staring her in the face.

She was coming toward him now. If she touched him, it would hurt.

Amy reached the couch, climbing onto his lap. She was searching between both his eyes, his good one and the one that might as well have been stitched closed. Her fingers touched his cheek, traveling over the ridges where the stitches had been removed two days ago. The skin underneath was sensitive, and it tickled slightly. Her fingers traced his non-existent hairline, the red surface, skin that came from somewhere else, shiny but sensitive to her smoothing motion, as if she could cure his cratered face.

Her fingers moved over to his lips. She leaned into him, her warm breasts against his cotton shirt taking his breath away. And then the miracle of miracles happened; she followed where her fingers had pressed, and she gave him the gift of her lips. Her tongue sought his. She drank from him, inhaling him as her body bloomed into full arousal while her fingertips still pressed lightly on his scars.

"Amy—I."

"Shh. I see you, Zak. I see all of you. I want all of you. I want you now."

"But I—" He couldn't speak because she was in his mouth again, sucking his tongue deep inside hers and then releasing him. She moved to his right, making small nibbles on his healed but puckered flesh, following the lines of the ridges of his repair. If kissing something could make it well, like his mother had done with him as a child, her kisses would surely heal him. She laid her flawless cheek against his. She kissed his earlobe, tugging on it with her teeth. Her tongue circled the arch of his outer ear, which had been untouched by the assassin's round. The liquid whisper she gave him set his soul on fire.

"Open your heart, Zak. Let me come in."

He felt her tears as she continued to whisper.

"I ache for you."

He brought his hand up, splaying his fingers through her hair; his other hand felt the soft texture of her perfect bottom beneath her jeans.

He stood, holding her with one hand beneath her rear, pressing her against him, her legs wrapped around his waist. She continued to kiss his flawed face, even to touch some of the healed patches with the tip of her tongue. He walked them to the bedroom. He laid her with all the tenderness he could muster, allowing her to fall back slowly into the cool cotton sheets. On his knees before her, she had two fingers in her mouth, her dark eyes calling to him in the unmistakable message of lust.

How could he be so lucky to have found someone so beautiful, someone who wanted him so deeply? She started to remove her top, and he stopped her.

"No. Let me do it. I want to do it all."

Her luscious smile had to be kissed. Her fingertips followed from the arch below his still-swollen eye, up along his temple and onto his body's fledgling re-growth of hair as he penetrated her mouth.

"Take me, Zak."

"Slowly, my love." It was the first word he'd used since coming back that gave him an emotional tag. She moaned and turned her head, exposing her long neck. He explored the wonder of its smoothness with his tongue then his fingers. Their kiss was still attached as he unbuttoned her fly, pushing the stubborn jeans down her hips.

Back to his knees, he held her ankles with one hand while he peeled her pants from her. He spread her flower with his fingers, pressing her clit with his thumb, then put his mouth on her and sucked the little bud stiff.

Her pelvis was undulating. He tucked his knees beneath her rear to raise her angle for feasting.

Amy's hair splayed over the pillow as she arched to

him. Her moans welcomed him. Her eyes and lips silently begged him. She moved to him, attempting to fill his mouth with her pussy.

He laid her back on the bed. Standing, he removed his own clothes quickly and came back to her with his erection looming above her. She was on her knees, taking him into her mouth, squeezing his sac gently, pulling down. He watched her head move on him, his fingers sifting through her hair. His confidence roared to life at the way she played his body. He closed his eyes and allowed himself to surrender to this woman.

Open your heart to me, Zak, she was saying non-verbally. It was painful to need someone so much, but he did need her more than he would be able to express. Maybe in a hundred more encounters, maybe then he could tell her. He'd learn. He wanted to learn all over again how to love her.

He lifted her head up, his hands beneath her jaw. Her hot lips sunk into his as they kneeled facing each other. Her hands stroked him, pulled at him. She took his hand and placed it at her sex, pushed on two fingers, inserting them inside her. He continued to fill her slippery channel until he laid her back on the bed. Both their hands together positioned him at her opening. They touched her lips as he joined with her. She clutched his butt cheeks and pulled him deep, holding him rigid and aching inside her.

One hand braced him against the mattress; the other held her arms above her head, stretching her torso long. But she arched up so that her breasts pressed against him with each thrust. His lips rubbed over her eyes, up the sides of her face, and down the delicate muscle extending below her ear. He bit her there, sucking her flesh until he tasted blood.

He watched her writhe beneath him, watched as the sexual glow of her eyes shone in the early evening and burned a hole of yearning right through him. His pumping continued until the familiar tightening in his sac announced the satisfying explosion that followed deep inside her.

His movements converted to long strokes as he spilled. She bit her lip, resisted his grip on her wrists, and then began to shatter. Her undulations squeezed his cock when he withdrew, unwilling to let him go. He pushed back inside her again, deeper still.

At last she arched, holding her breath. Her orgasm splashed over them both. He kissed her until her silky body settled into a low burn.

He released her arms, kissing her wrists. Her eyes followed his every movement. Her smile was distant, lurking somewhere close to naughty. Her fingers touched his face and traced tears he didn't realize had fallen in large streaks down his cheeks.

"This is all of me, Amy. Such as I am." He held her

palm and tenderly kissed it.

"This is all I am, Zak," she said. "I am yours forever. No matter what."

This was the part of loving Amy he could stay immersed in forever.

CHAPTER 23

EARLY OCTOBER WAS beautiful in Sonoma County, so Zak and Amy decided to take a trip up to wine country and visit her dad and his parents. The prospect of staying in the Chief's big house, even with Marlene to do interference, was barely considered. They had a favorite place in mind.

He was about to put his bandage on, preparing for the drive north.

"Is it my imagination or does it look better this morning, Zak?"

He stopped, peering back at her in the mirror, returning her examination of his face. "Wish it was that easy, Amy. But it does feel less tight, and I'm beginning to have some sensation on my cheek. Not the same as my left one, but something anyway."

"Do they recommend something for the healing? Like a Vitamin E cream for the scarring now that there are no more open wounds and the stitches have been removed?"

"The Navy? You think the Navy would recommend Vitamin E?" Though the right side of his cheek bulged out unnaturally and his smile was off kilter, she saw his sense of humor was returning.

"Let me try something." In one of the bathroom drawers, she found some Vitamin E infused with lavender oil. "Lavender is supposed to be good for scarring, as well as the vitamin E." She unscrewed the small black cap and poured a tiny amount the size of a dime into the palm of her hand. The heady aroma from the lavender was relaxing as she dipped her fingers in the reservoir in her palm and applied it carefully to his face with the beds of her first two fingers. "It is better, Zak."

He replaced the bandage. This time, Amy helped him make strips of tape for attaching the mask to his face. Her fingers pressed the bandage around the bridge of his nose, taking care not to allow any air gaps for aid in healing.

Outside Santa Rosa and toward the town of Sonoma was the Waterwheel Inn, well known to lovers world-wide. It was an extravagant idea, but they decided to start their new life in the beauty of the little boutique inn, booking a room near the slowly turning namesake: the waterwheel. The room was generous, with a roaring fireplace ten feet from the foot of their king-sized bed.

Within minutes, he had her undressed and considering not going to see her father at all, but staying in the lovely Inn. By firelight, his face was softer, the orange glow reflected well on his skin, minimizing the lines of sutures. His right eyelid was nearly normal in size, but the eye inside was still bloodshot.

She watched him kiss down the middle of her upper torso, lips nibbling a moist trail down to the juncture between her legs. As he pleasured her, she closed her eyes, unable to focus on anything but giving herself up to him. She was grateful he'd found that part of himself that allowed for experimentation and excitement in their bedroom again.

It was wonderful to have him back at last.

THEY VISITED CHIEF Dobson just after a long breakfast in bed. Zak was forgetting to put the face patch on more and more, but for these visits, he presented himself to her so she could press the adhesive tape into the bridge of his nose, his hairline above his eye, and in front of his ear. Investigating the position of the bandage, she searched for gaps and found none.

At first, Amy's dad shook his hand nervously without making eye contact. Marlene watched warily, but eventually, their conversation over strong coffee fell on what their future beheld.

"I'm going to see what happens with the eye. There's a man up here who trained a friend of mine when he lost his eye. Hell of a teacher. I've asked him to take me to the range."

This surprised even Amy. "When did you talk to him?"

"I called just before we left. He said he'd be glad to give me some pointers, some things to practice."

"Never heard anyone learning to change their dominant shooting sights. Can that be done?" Dobson asked.

"We'll see."

"So are you going back to the teams, Zak?" Marlene wanted to know.

"If they'll have me, yes."

Why hasn't he mentioned this? He seemed to have lots of little secrets, things he kept private, and this bothered her. Did he not trust her with the truth of what he was planning?

Zak turned to her. "You remember Kelly, the lady I introduced you to at Coop's barbeque?"

Amy began to understand what he was talking about. "You mean the one who was married to your friend before—"

"Yes, before he was killed. Roger taught him to shoot with his right eye. Joel was a leftie before. She's the one who gave me Roger's phone number."

She listened to him tell the tale to her dad and Marlene, how the SEAL had lost his eye, requalified expert, and was allowed to rejoin his old team, even though the Navy had tried to medically discharge him.

Joel's journey was identical to Zak's new mission, Amy thought.

Her dad's post-heart attack schedule was wearing well on him, Amy thought. His relaxed face smiled more. She noted the closeness he and Marlene shared and was happy for him. It also released a burden from her shoulders.

NEXT, THEY WENT over to Zak's parents, who pummeled him with lots of questions. The concern his mother wore on her face, her probing about his care and the treatments he was being given annoyed Amy a little. Gloria Dobson barely noted her presence, she was so wrapped up in her son.

"You and I should try shooting while you're up here. Had an old friend who learned to shoot with his non-dominant eye when he lost the other one to Diabetes. I know it can be done."

"See, Amy?" Zak was encouraged. Then he turned back to his dad. "Better let me meet with Roger first, see what he says."

"Roger?"

"Remember when Joel lost his eye?"

"The SEAL you played soccer with?"

"Yes."

"God, I forgot all about that, Zak. So you think this guy can help you?"

"It's worth a shot. Otherwise, I have none. I'm useless to the Teams."

"But will they allow you to stay on?" his mother asked.

"They let Joel back. Remember?"

Amy let him recount the story. She picked up on a stronger connection with Joel and his wife this time. Joel was almost like the older brother Zak had never had. His death had happened during one of their numerous dating breaks, when she was still in high school and Zak was trying very hard to flunk out of college.

ZAK WAS UNUSUALLY quiet on the way home.

"You okay?"

"Yup. I definitely saw light tonight, Amy. I think perhaps my vision, some of it anyway, is coming back."

"Seriously? That's so wonderful. Oh, what a miracle." She leaned into him, resting her head on his shoulder. He withdrew his arm from the steering wheel and wrapped it around her shoulders.

"I don't want to get my hopes up too far, but I take it as a very good sign. I didn't see anything I could make out, but I definitely did see flashes of light."

CHAPTER 24

Z AK HAD HIS shooting lesson with Roger the next day. He sold him a left-handed Sig Sauer, and the adjustment wasn't as difficult as he'd anticipated. The long gun was a whole other thing.

After returning to Coronado, he continued to have streams of light flash across his right eye on a daily basis, but the headaches were back, and he still couldn't make out any shapes.

He went to the range every day, sometimes spending nearly the whole day there. He avoided the heavy lifting with the rest of the team on workout days, but did participate in inlet swims, which didn't affect his headaches or cause pressure on his eye.

The doctors were encouraged with his progress as the weeks went by. Pam stretched and manipulated him into knots, giving him deep tissue massages after their sessions. His balance improved. She tested his eyesight, and his one eye got stronger as his brain mentally compensated for the lack of depth perception.

He finally was coming into the range of accuracy he had before the injury. It still didn't feel natural to use his less-dominant left eye, but he was reworking the neural pathways. He got permission to do more physical training, starting with some TRX work on his arms, legs, and abs, but he was still cautioned not to do pullups, situps, or pushups—nothing that would put pressure on his eye.

Light continued to brighten, but the eye was still useless for seeing shapes. Trying to focus and make his eye perform gave him headaches and frustrated him, but he wouldn't quit. It drove him further. He made an appointment for testing to re-qualify as Expert. Carter and others encouraged him to take more time, to be fully ready before taking the test. If he failed, he might not even be considered to come back to the Teams. Even if he passed, there was the possibility the Navy would still decide to medically discharge him.

After workouts, he frequently hung out at the Scupper with Carter and Alex, who was now fully healed. Alex had gone through several girlfriends in the short weeks since they'd been back.

"I'm looking for an Amy," Alex said one evening.

"Those are fighting words, my man," barked Carter. "Jell-O here's one helluva shot now. I'd watch your tongue."

"I don't want Amy. I just want someone like her. She's always so nice to be around. She smiles."

"You have to treat women nice before you get that kind of result, Alex. Your problem is that you don't listen. All of us who've been married—happily married, I might add—have been saying this all along." Zak saw Alex arch at the insult.

"I treat women nice. I'm attracted to the headstrong ones, I guess."

"No." Zak had Alex pegged. "You're attracted to the ones who won't commit because that makes it easier for you."

Late one afternoon, as he was driving home from practice, he got a call from Kelly. He agreed to stop by to see her when she tearfully admitted her engagement had been called off.

She met him at the door in cutoffs and a pink Punisher tee shirt. Her eyes were nearly the same color.

She poured him a glass of wine and he declined. "Not drinking anymore, Kelly. I'll just take some water."

She brought him a glass with lots of ice and dropped to the couch, tucking her legs underneath her. "God, Zak, I've been such an idiot."

"Did he hurt you?"

"No, not physically. We're just not a good fit. We fight all the time, I mean *all* the time." Her bright blue eyes searched his face, making note of the bandage he still wore. "When do you take that off?"

"I have at least two more surgeries this year. Then perhaps I'll be able to."

"Isn't it taking a long time to heal?"

"No. I'm healed. I just like to keep it covered. It's easier for people that way. There's a lot of scaring down here and up into my hairline." He indicated all this with his forefinger.

"Joel was lucky that way. It was a bullet fragment that lodged in his eye. I thought his patch was kind of sexy. Of course, he didn't take it so well."

"I'll bet. He was an amazing warrior. He had more kills than anyone in the history of the Navy. He was a good guy."

"I miss him, Zak. I just don't think anyone could take his place. He fought so hard. They wanted to roll him, and he argued and argued with the Navy." She smiled, examining her hands. "In the end they made him do the BUD/S class all over again. But he did it."

Zak found himself feeling uncomfortable and began to wish he'd never come over. He was not the one who should be here with Kelly just breaking up with her fiancé.

He decided to change the subject. "Tell me how he did it. I know he worked with Roger, and some others. Did he ever get any light or sensation from that one bad eye?"

"Never. He kept hoping it would. He'd feel like something was changing inside, and he got his hopes up all the time. *Today's the day, Kelly,* he said. He worked so hard he got down on himself when he didn't feel he was progressing fast enough."

She shrugged, twirling her hair and making Zak feel even more uncomfortable. "They didn't give him any breaks with the ration of crap they threw at him every day. After he'd survived and passed BUD/S again, he was a different man."

"I can only imagine."

"He'd missed his rotation, so to avoid getting cut, after he graduated BUD/S, he joined another team, as you know."

"The body does what the body does," Zak said, quoting his doctor in Landstuhl.

She eyed him then broke out into a grin. "Amy's nice, Zak."

"We were high school sweethearts."

"I like that. I miss that. Someone to play around with. The long showers and sleep-ins. Walking the beach under the stars. Being romantic. Joel and I had that."

She gave him an honest glimpse of her pain and loneliness. Her eyes searched him for answers. "Do you ever think I'll find that again? It would have to be another SEAL. I've been through the dark days when he was first injured. I know how that works."

He was dangerously charmed and felt bad about it, but he told himself he did feel sorry for her loss. Even though it was undeniable that there was some chemistry between them, she was free and he was not.

"Kelly, I'd better go."

"Yes. You should."

Zak thought about their encounter all the way home and decided he'd never go see Kelly again. And he'd never tell Amy.

SHE WAS WAITING in the darkened living room when he returned.

"What's wrong?"

"Why didn't you call me? You said you were on your way home. I made dinner, and then I waited over an hour. No Zak. No phone call. I left you messages."

He pulled his cell out and checked and sure enough there were those messages from Amy, but the phone was on silent.

"I'm sorry. I had it turned off at the—" He realized his lie. Kelly called him. He'd turned it off when he was at her house and didn't notice Amy's call and texts. "Sweetheart, I'm sorry."

"At the what?"

"I made a stop on the way home, that's all."

"Where?"

He didn't want to lie to her, but he knew she would never understand. "I just drove around. I kicked some tires. I bought an ice cream and went down to the beach. I just needed to think, Amy. That's all."

He knew he'd be in serious trouble if she found out about the lie, but he'd made a huge mistake in judgment, and he didn't want her to know. He was ashamed of himself.

"Maybe you don't notice it, but ever since you've been on this kick with the marksman stuff, you're gone most of the day. We don't talk. You spend more time with your team buddies than you do me."

"I'm sorry, Amy. I really am."

"It isn't fair, Zak."

"You're right, of course." He slipped next to her on the couch, leaning shoulder against shoulder with her, as she hunched over her knees and studied the carpet. "I'm trying to keep my spot on the Team, if I can. I'm doing everything I can to do that, sweetheart."

"But I'm secondary."

Here it was again. He had to make a decision. But first, he had to clarify something with Amy.

"Sweetheart, nothing has changed. I need to know, are you with me going back on the Teams? I need to know that. It's like when I asked you this before we got married. It's the same question now, honey."

He was encouraged when she nodded her head. He rubbed the back of her neck. "I'm trying to be honest with you."

"Are you happy, Zak?"

He was getting annoyed with her questions and her tone. "You know I'm happy, and I'm working hard. They might ask me to go through BUD/S and requalify again."

She frowned. "They do that?"

"Apparently, sometimes."

"Would you pass?"

"What, you think I'm some weakling and couldn't get through it?"

"But you're not training hard. You have to still be careful with your eye."

"Which is why I'll wait until I get released, and then I'll know. I want to be ready. I'm getting there. I'm getting better every day."

"I need to ask you something, Zak."

"Shoot."

"I want to go look for work. I'm kind of going stir crazy here, waiting on you hand and foot, being on-call between your appointments. With the uncertainty of you going back, I think I need to get a job. Maybe start selling real estate with Christy."

He hadn't thought about Amy's needs. He'd been so focused on his own plan, he'd not considered hers.

Their showing affection for each other had waned. She was right about that. He didn't feel less for her; she just seemed not to be interested. And yes, he was gone most of the time. She'd drill him full of questions about all his appointments, and he'd started resenting it. She was always there for him. But he showed up when he could. That wasn't fair.

"Go for it, sweetheart."

"Really?" She threw her arms around him.

"Of course. I'm strong now. You helped get me there."

CHAPTER 25

AMY'S BACKGROUND IN sales at the Omni in San Francisco made her uniquely qualified for the Millenium Waterfront complex near the boat harbor and convention center in downtown San Diego. Even during her first week on the job, she managed to sell one of the most expensive townhomes to a family from Dubai.

The all-cash offer was transacted in as short a timeframe as possible. The family was buying it for their son who was already attending college there. Her six figure check was thrilling to hold in her hand. Since it was her day off, she decided to go surprise Zak at the gym where he was working out.

Gunny's Gym was the team favorite for most the San Diego teams. Although Gunny had passed on, his son and one of his legally married wives, a beautiful Thai woman named Amornpan, ran the place. Though the equipment was old and occasionally rusty, everything was clean. She'd brought in an acupuncturist and a massage therapist. A picture of the old Gunnery Sergeant was hung in a red frame with gold trim prominently above the mirror behind the desk. Amy imagined the SEALs swore to him when their workouts hurt and said a prayer before deployments. He'd been a fixture of the community, and he still lived in their hearts.

Amornpan greeted Amy. "Zak is not here today."

Amy frowned. "What?" She checked her phone. No message.

"Kyle came running in saying something about this guy on Team 5 coming to the clinic today. He's just back from Germany, like your Zak."

"Oh, so they're coming back, then?"

The attractive woman shrugged. "I hope so. But they all took their bags. So I think not."

"Is he going to be okay?"

"I think so. They play some joke on him, I think. You know those guys. Always playing jokes."

Amy knew this to be typical team behavior. They'd make up their workout later, but they never passed up a chance to get into a little mischief. "Thank you."

"My pleasure, missie. Have good day."

Amy raced to the clinic about twenty minutes away. Across the inlet, large grey ships were lined up like cows in a barn. She'd spent a lot of time looking out the clinic windows at their goings and comings. Two cruise ships dotted the other side of the bay, their white hulls glistening in the San Diego sun.

She found Zak's Hummer and parked next to it in case she missed him.

Inside the reception area, the desk wasn't manned. Someone had spilled a coffee cup to the right, and it was resting against the vinyl tiled floor with its contents still traveling.

This just happened.

She heard some shouting coming from behind a closed door down the hallway. Several women screamed. And then she heard the unmistakable sound of automatic gunfire.

Where's Zak? Was he in that room?

The door swung open. White smoke billowed out into the hallway. Two armed men, dressed in black, including black knit facemasks, ran from the room. Upon spying her, despite her efforts to duck around a corner, they quickly overtook her. One man held her wrists behind her waist and pulled a ziplock tie from his pocket, securing her arms together behind her, rendering her completely defenseless.

Her next worry was that they would use the weapon on her. The two men spoke in broken English with two different accents. One sounded German and the other Arabic.

The gunman who had secured her wrists together yanked her by the zip ties. She had been turned around and was walking backwards quickly to avoid falling and thereby incur their wrath. She searched for some evidence others were nearby, and then she smelled the food and realized they were close to the cafeteria. It was nearly noon. The place would be packed.

The masked gunmen pulled her into the doorway of the cafeteria, which drew screams from several women there. The gunmen fired rounds into the ceiling. "You will stand over here if you are military." He pointed to an area near a huge silver frozen yogurt machine. "If you are civilian, you stand here," the gunman said as he pointed with the end of his medium-sized automatic weapon.

A furtive glance amongst the crowd didn't yield any faces she recognized except for the physical therapist, Pam, who began moving in the direction of the civilian crowd. Amy knew she was still military.

Several men and women wore scrubs over camo pants and shirts and shuffled slowly, not going to either camp. The other gunman shot one of the men who had hesitated with a short burst of automatic fire, the man's head exploding before their eyes as his torso dropped to the ground.

Why are they holding me?

"You will separate now or I will kill you all."

That's when Amy noticed the bulge waist height underneath the oversized black nylon jacket. He turned to face her. "Military or civilian?"

"Civilian," she answered.

The other gunman shouted to the man who had Amy by the wrist ties, and she was pushed ahead of them toward the cafeteria entrance. She was in the hallway as she saw the other gunman adopt a stance she'd seen Zak take when he was firing his M-4. The room was going to be sprayed with rounds, and everyone would be killed.

She didn't know what to do except scream. Taking a deep breath, thinking it might be her very last one, she decided to make it count.

"Z-a-a-a-k!" she yelled at the top of her lungs, surprising herself how loud and forceful she sounded. The gunmen had not expected her outburst. She was too close to them to have them fire upon her without hitting each other.

A single shot came from the cafeteria, taking one gunman out with a loud thud, followed by the blood spray from the man's forehead as he dropped.

The remaining gunman let loose of her just as she saw he was angling to cover the room in fire. A split second later, she heard Zak's voice. "Drop, Amy, now."

And that's what she did. She dove for the vinyl tile floor, the forward momentum sending her sliding five feet toward the direction of Zak's voice. With another double tap, the last gunman's chest and neck exploded, covering her with his blood.

And then it was silent. Inside the cafeteria, someone was asking if there were only two shooters. Amy heard boots running down the hallway. With her arms outstretched like she was attempting to land on her belly, she arched up to see who was running straight for her.

Zak's white bandage was hanging at an angle, exposing much of his scared face for all to see. As he pulled her to her feet and embraced her, Zak didn't pay attention to the condition of his face, his bandage, or the light spray of blood covering her. He held her tightly in powerful arms like he would never let her go.

CHAPTER 26

WITHOUT THE WEAPONS training Zak had been doing almost daily, the unexpected sight of Amy might have caused hesitation, which could have proven fatal to not only himself but the hostages.

Acutely aware what danger they were in, he'd aimed for the gunman's head and missed. But he downed the man anyway, hitting him square in the chest and neck.

"What in the world are you doing here?"

"I—I—c-came to show you my check?" It sounded more like a question because it was so absurd.

"What check?"

"My commission check. It's huge, Zak. I came to brag. To thank you for letting—"

Zak covered her mouth with his, cutting off any ridiculous thing she was about to say. She was shaking. Zak pulled her harder still against him. She smelled his favorite lemon spiced cologne, mixed with the unmistakable scent of his sweat. As he clutched the hair at the back of her head, forcing her lips against his mouth, she felt the warm beads of perspiration on his upper lip. And she felt herself melt into him.

She was soon surrounded by Kyle and Armando and several others from Team 3, including Alex, who winked at her.

"How're we doing kids, huh? Wasn't that fun?" he said mimicking a television commercial.

Amy was aware her heart was pounding against her chest. Her ears were starting to tune into one high-pitched hissing sound. Kyle walked over to the gunman who'd had her by the wrists.

Amy broke out of Zak's embrace. "Kyle! Wait! We should evacuate the building. I think he has a belt. Something around his waist."

The SEALs quickly ordered everyone out to the parking lot in front. Armando and Fredo did a quick sweep of the area, making sure there weren't any carloads of explosives or other shooters waiting. They found none.

Kyle advanced on Amy and Zak, locked in an embrace. "Good shot, Jell-O. If you'd missed, and hit the belt instead, we all wouldn't be here now."

"I did miss. I was aiming for his head. I got his chest and neck."

"That's the best fuckin' kind of miss I've ever seen,

frogman." To the rest of his squad and some of the nurses, he yelled, "Someone call the police. Who's a doctor here?"

"So what were you guys doing here?" she asked.

→"Daryl from SEAL Team 5 was getting fit for his prosthetic. Coop made him a peg leg with lasers and lights, like his arm toy. We came by to see the therapist present it to him." Zak followed it up with a shrug.

"Course, before we could fully judge his reaction, we heard the shooting. Man, Amy, you seem to attract the bad buys," Kyle said.

"Yeah, bad in all the right ways." Zak grabbed Amy and gave her a kiss.

THEY GAVE REPORTS to the police as rescue workers began to arrive. Afterward, Zak followed Amy home.

"I've given it a lot of thought, Amy. It's not fair for you if I go back. If you don't want me to, I'll stop trying to make the Team again. You were right to point this out. I don't want you to be number two. You're my number one."

Amy grinned, but couldn't look him in the eye.

"What?" he asked.

"I made a decision too. Being a SEAL is who you are. So we fight. Like your Ethos says, we fight to win, not to play. You are that man, Zak. You are a SEAL. Now we just have to get the Navy to understand that."

He wasn't sure what to do. Zak hadn't expected her words.

"I said I wasn't a quitter. Now's not the time to start. I say we go for it. If we don't make it, then we decide what else we want to do. It's a *we* thing, sweetheart. We do this together."

There weren't enough kisses in the world to thank her for what she'd just given him. And although it would be tough, he was going to try to achieve that mission too.

CHAPTER 27

TWO MONTHS AFTER their mission to protect the Secretary of State, the Coopers were having another barbeque. It was a Halloween costume party, especially for the little kids, who would not be allowed out in the neighborhood trick-or-treating.

Amy was in her pirate wench costume, waiting for Zak to come out so they could leave for the party. New reports were still buzzing over the fact that only a handful of clinic personnel had been murdered by the terrorists who apparently had planned to blow up the whole facility. Not understanding it was a drop-in clinic, it was speculated they were expecting to see hospital beds filled with active military and retired vets. The cafeteria was their best chance to get a large number of kills in one place.

Amy had come in at just the right time. A few minutes before, she'd have been part of the pile of bodies in the room off the hallway. A couple of minutes later, she would have heard the spray of gunfire as the occupants of the cafeteria were mowed down. Or perhaps she'd walk in just in time to leave this earth in a cloud of explosives.

So her timing was perfect. The newscaster said the hospital security staff, not mentioning the SEALs, had defied orders and brought weapons to the site and that's how so many lives were saved. Unlike other recent shootings and attacks on military personnel and their families all over the world, this attack was foiled because the people responsible for protection of the innocent were trained and armed and not afraid to use their weapons. They were heralded as heroes.

This drew a smile to her lips. Some real-life security guard was about to get a medal for something the SEALs did, but that was the way of it. Armando had been the shooter in the cafeteria while Zak took down the one in the hallway.

The bedroom door was closed, and Zak was being very quiet. He'd been secretive all day, unwilling to tell her about his costume. She halfway expected he'd dress up in something outrageous. She'd asked, and none of the other wives or guys knew what he'd bought.

"Zak?" She said loud enough to penetrate the door and listened for an answer from him. "I thought you never liked to be late."

She sat down in the overstuffed chair she had

learned to love more every day. She flipped off the television.

The door opened. His voice preceded him into the room. His costume swished as he appeared before her.

He was dressed in a starched white shirt and tux, a red bow tie at his neck. His hair was gelled back and smooth. Over the tux, he wore a black satin cape tied under his chin. His shoes were polished to a perfect shine. He wore white gloves.

He would have looked like an elegant vampire, except for one thing. Over his right eye, extending down his cheek, back to the front of his ear and over the bare patch of scalp was a white half-mask of form-fitting plastic.

He was the sexiest Phantom she'd ever seen.

"Oh my God, Zak! It's perfect!"

"Why, Christine, you have Carlotta's costume on."

"Oh dear. Should I take it off now or...?"

He bent down, brushing her lips with his, whispering, "Later, but I won't be able to think about anything else until then. You will have me in agony all evening."

"Good. You deserve it. You've made us late for the party."

ALEX WAS DRESSED as Robin Hood and accompanied one of the nurses from the clinic he'd met two days ago. Kyle was a pirate and insisted he get a picture with both Amy and Christy, his wenches.

Fredo was dressed as one ugly, rotund Mexican woman with one of his mother-in-law's embroidered dresses and Mia's bra stuffed with foam. Libby was a fairy queen, and their daughter was a fairy princess. All three of Kyle's kids, two boys and a girl, were pirates to match their dad. Coop didn't dress up at all.

"Someone's got to look normal," he mumbled, chewing on ice.

Zak's costume was the most popular by far.

Music played for those who wanted to dance under the stars in the Cooper's backyard. Amidst little people tripping over costumes and playing with imaginary plastic swords and sabers, Zak and Amy danced a slow dance. Amy barely heard the ruckus around them.

The air was chilly, and she shivered.

"You cold, my dear?"

"No; in your arms I'm never cold, my love. I'm moved by your countenance, the way our bodies sway back and forth. I'm thinking of how nicely they move together in bed, too."

"Shh. Little ears are listening, I fear."

"Nothing is going to keep me from enjoying this night." She placed her cheek against his shirt and heard the beating of his heart. He wrapped the protection of the cape around her shoulders as they moved slowly, turning first one way, and then the other, avoiding children, dogs, and candy wrappers covering the backyard.

It had been a magical evening. She'd had a little too much champagne to drink, so she leaned into him more than she normally did as they walked to the Hummer.

On the way home, Zak missed a turn.

"What are you doing?" Amy asked.

"It's a surprise."

In the shadows of the late night, Amy soon saw where they were headed. He parked the truck and they walked hand in hand across the parking lot. They found a small gap in the wrought iron fencing just wide enough to let them through. Once onto the green, Zak removed his cape, spread it out, sat, and extended his hand to Amy.

"My love. Join me?"

Amy was on her knees in front of him so fast he began to chuckle.

"Mrs. Chambers, I do believe you are quite randy!" he said in a mock English accent.

"My panties are soaked."

"Ahh, just what the Phantom wants to hear!" He kissed her palm. "I have a confession to make."

"What?"

"I never told you that green is my favorite color—for walls. For golf courses. Whenever I see green, I get hard."

"Green? Zak, that's so silly. I would never think that."

"Well, you have not seen what I have seen on green lawns, my dear," he said as he wiggled his eyebrows.

"Ah. What's your other favorite color?"

He turned her head to the side, kissed her ear, and whispered, "Pink. I like all your pink places, Amy."

A shiver went down her spine. The erotic blush happening between her legs gave her a dull ache in the pit of her stomach. Zak was on his knees. He looked up at her, his mask still in place as he slowly removed his white gloves and laid them beside her.

One by one, he lifted her petticoats. He searched the inside of her thigh until he came to the elastic edge of her panties. She felt the roughness of his fingers as they breached the elastic and found the wet lips of her sex. He slid easily into her.

Amy placed her hands on his shoulders and arched back. His gentle push moved her knees more to the sides. With a quick flip of the petticoats, his head was beneath her skirt and his hot tongue was seeking a taste of her goodness. She could feel the mast rubbing against her thigh. Once he found her, he flicked over her clit as his lips covered her, sucking and exploring all her soft folds.

Her insides were on fire. Her nipples hardened and

sought release. The soft hairs at the back of her neck stood to attention. His kiss and touch in the most intimate of her places were bringing on the wild horses of arousal.

He feasted for several minutes before he came up for air, her juices on his lips. His mask was crooked. "Come. Let's get nekked."

"This is always the way I wished the Phantom could have ended. He should have gotten the girl," she said.

"I think so, too."

Zak removed her cotton blouse and her skirts, while Amy slipped off her shoes and the rest of her underwear. Then she helped him take off his black slacks, the shirt, and his American Flag boxers.

In the moonlight, the white mask of his costume shone with a paranormal glow. She removed it by stretching the elastic band and tossing it over her shoulder.

Her fingers explored the pebbled flesh of his face, now becoming smoother as it healed. She pulled on his earlobes with her thumbs and first two fingers, rose to her tiptoes, and kissed him.

Then she kissed his injured eye.

As they slid to the ground, her thighs parted, and she felt his stiff cock rooting between her legs until it snagged itself on her opening. With bold, smooth strokes, he pressed in deep.

The rhythm built. He angled, holding her thigh over his shoulder, and moved back and forth easily as her muscles squeezed him. Zak withdrew and sucked on her bud, sending electric pulses up her spine. Thrusting forward, he guided his cock while pressing her bud with his thumb, forcing it down with a delicious ache that generated spasms deep within her.

Her Phantom quickly flipped her over and held her pelvis up with his powerful hand as he entered her from behind. He pushed deeper still. His hips moved fluidly, raising her body up and down on him.

Amy moved her thighs outside his as she rocked her pelvis, rose, and fell down around him until the burn inside enveloped her whole body, her orgasm turning her liquid.

She didn't know what future was in store for them. She didn't know whether he'd ever regain the use of his right eye. If anyone could do it, Zak could. And whatever he decided, she'd be right there beside him.

Her man was flesh and blood. He was the one who came home, came back to her. He was no phantom. He was real.

They would heal each other.

The End

ABOUT THE AUTHOR

NYT and USA Today best-selling author Sharon Hamilton's award-winning Navy SEAL Brotherhood series have been a fan favorite from the day the first one was released. They've earned her the coveted Amazon author ranking of #1 in Romantic Suspense, Military Romance and Contemporary Romance categories, as well as in Gothic Romance for her Vampires of Tuscany and Guardian Angels. Her characters follow a sometimes rocky road to redemption through passion and true love.

Her Golden Vampires of Tuscany are not like any vamps you've read about before, since they don't go to ground and can walk around in the full light of the sun.

Her Guardian Angels struggle with the human charges they are sent to save, often escaping their vanilla world of Heaven for the brief human one. You won't find any of these beings in any Sunday school class.

She lives in Sonoma County, California with her husband and two Dobermans. A lifelong organic gardener, when she's not writing, she's getting *verra*

verra dirty in the mud, or wandering Farmers Markets looking for new Heirloom varieties of vegetables and flowers.

She loves hearing from her fans:

sharonhamilton2001@gmail.com

Her website is:

www.authorsharonhamilton.com

Find out more about Sharon, her upcoming releases, appearances and news from her newsletter.

authorsharonhamilton.com/contact.php#mailing-list

Sharon's Blog:

sharonhamiltonauthor.blogspot.com

Facebook:

facebook.com/SharonHamiltonAuthor

Twitter:

@sharonlhamilton

Life is one fool thing after another.
Love is two fool things after each other.

NAVY SEAL PRAYER

"Dear FATHER IN HEAVEN,

If I may respectfully say so sometimes you are a strange God. Though you love all mankind,

It seems you have special predilections too.

You seem to love those men who can stand up alone who face impossible odds, Who challenge every bully and every tyrant ~

Those men who know the heat and loneliness of Calvary. Possibly you cherish men of this stamp because you recognize the mark of your only son in them.

Since this unique group of men known as the SEALs know Calvary and suffering, teach them now the mystery of the resurrection ~ that they are indestructible, that they will live forever because of their deep faith in you.

And when they do come to heaven, may I respectfully warn you, Dear Father, they also know how to celebrate. So please be ready for them when they insert under your pearly gates.

Bless them, their devoted Families and their Country on this glorious occasion.

We ask this through the merits of your Son, Christ Jesus the Lord, Amen."

By Reverend E.J. McMalhon S.J. LCDR, CHC, USN
Awards Ceremony SEAL Team One
1975 At NAB, Coronado

Made in the USA
Middletown, DE
26 September 2018